ALWAYS KIND OF LOVE

A MCCORD FAMILY NOVEL
BOOK 4

AMANDA SIEGRIST

McCord Family Novel

Protecting You

Trust in Love

Deserving You

Always Kind of Love

Finding You

Dare You to Love

Mona & Mason

The Paranormal Chronicles, Volume 1

Perfect For You Novel

The Wrong Brother

The Right Time

The Easy Part

The Hard Choice

Psychic Love Novel

Exploding Love

Captured Love

Slaying Love Novel

Won't Let You Go

Doomed Love

Deadly Crazy

Evidence of Sin

Finding Redemption

Obsessed Hope

Short Stories

Paint By Murder

Follow Me, Sweet Darling

Sleighville Novel

Dashing Through the Fear

Here Comes Chaos

The Last Noel

Standalone Novel

The Danger with Love

Conquering Fear Novel

CO-WRITTEN WITH JANE BLYTHE

Drowning in You

Out of the Darkness

Closing In

I hope you enjoy book 4 in my **McCord Family Novel series**. This story is a bit shorter than the first three books, but that's because it was a part of the Risking Everything: A Steamy Anthology of First Responders. We had a word count we had to adhere to. All proceeds went to the charity - the Stephen Siller Tunnel to Towers Foundation.

You'll also notice at the beginning of chapter 1 I have a writing prompt noted. That's because the very first scene in Ethan's point of view was written during one of my weekly flash fiction, something I used to love to write every Friday!

Happy reading!
🩶 Much love, Amanda Siegrist

1

WRITING PROMPT ~ HEARTS AND SLOPPY KISSES...

Do you really want to test me?

That wasn't generally a question he was asked. And when it did pop up, as it had about five minutes ago, his immediate response was, "No way."

Ethan McCord wasn't an idiot. He generally went with the flow. Not much upset him; he could usually find the humor in any situation. What was the point of getting upset? And, Deja, his sister-in-law, could skewer a person with one scorching look with her bright blue eyes. He never wanted to test that particular demon.

So, when she asked him to stop by the office to pick up the paperwork she'd left sitting on her desk—and he hesitated—it prompted a stern gaze from her, and he automatically answered with, "Of course."

In reality, he just wanted to go home, relax, and have a beer. His last shift at work hadn't been a good one. He'd slept all morning into the afternoon, trying to recover from yesterday's grueling day.

But Emmett, his brother, was working late, and Deja insisted she needed those papers before tomorrow, but she was cooking and couldn't leave the house. Why she couldn't ask Emmett, her husband, who would gladly swing by the office and pick it up, was beyond him.

Sometimes it was easier to let it go. It wouldn't take him more than twenty minutes out of his routine to grab her stuff. Then he could veg out in front of the TV with a cold one and decompress.

Pulling into the parking lot where Emmett rented a building for his landscaping business, he parked right next to a small, red vehicle.

Odd.

It was late. Almost eight o'clock and all the businesses were closed for the day. No other vehicles should've been around.

Of course, that wasn't what he found odd.

The car itself looked weirdly familiar. But he couldn't pinpoint why.

Shaking his head, afraid he was losing his mind from the tiring day, he got out of the truck, grabbed his spare key, and swiftly made an entrance.

He didn't bother turning on the lights since Deja said the stack of papers she needed would be sitting on the corner of her desk. Except when he walked the few steps from the front door to her desk, he didn't see a damn thing.

A clean desk. Obsessively clean. Nothing out of place. The computer was shut off. All the pens and pencils were sitting in a white cup next to the keyboard, a small notepad next to it. Nothing else littered the desk.

Deja was a neat freak when it came to her workspace. She kept everything orderly and very organized. So if she said the papers would be on the corner of her desk, they should've been.

Maybe she meant Emmett's desk. He turned around and

paused when he saw a splash of yellow light peeking out from underneath Emmett's office door.

Shit.

Someone broke in.

Probably the same someone who parked right in front of the building.

Were they that dumb? Why would they park right in front of the building and break in?

And how did they break in? The door was locked. No windows appeared to be broken.

Plunk!

Ethan took a step forward when he heard the muffled sound of something falling.

He knew he should call the police, but he didn't know how long the suspect had been in the building and they could walk out of the office at any moment. Better if he caught them off guard instead of the other way around.

Shoving his keys in his pocket, he grabbed an umbrella from the cute umbrella holder Sophie, his cousin Austin's wife, made out of old pieces of wood, then wrapped his hands around it with a tight grip. He might not be a cop, but he was a firefighter, and he could hold his own. The police department was right next to the fire department, and he worked out all the time with some of the other cops. He knew how to take down a suspect.

He'd restrain the perp, then call the cops.

Heart pounding a fraction, he grabbed the door handle and swung it open, the umbrella high in the air.

The umbrella arched down.

A scream rented the air.

Then a hard object hit him squarely in the face, right in the cheek, almost hitting his left eye.

"Shit." The umbrella immediately fell from his hand as he covered his face with his arm.

"Ethan?"

He pressed the back of his hand lightly to his cheek, checking to see if he could feel any blood. Whatever it was that hit him had hit hard. He stared, dumbfounded, at the woman standing a few feet away.

Well, damn.

That's why the red car looked familiar.

And not in a good way.

"Penelope." Just saying her name sent a shiver rushing down his spine.

"What are you doing here?"

His brows rose in surprise, which in turn made him cringe from the ache in his cheek. "Me? What the hell are you doing here? How did you get in?"

She pointed a long finger at him, her nails painted a bright, shiny red. "How did *you* get in here?"

"With a key." He patted his pocket, then reached up and rubbed his cheek. It hurt. He could honestly use that cold one right about now, and not to drink, but to press it against his wound.

Her expression changed from confused anger to concerned worry in a flash. Within three large steps, she stood right in front of him and cupped his cheek and tilted his head.

Like she had some right to touch him.

"Oh, I'm so sorry. You startled me whipping open the door like that, and I threw the first thing in my reach."

Ethan tried to control his breathing with her soft hands on his face. Oh, the delicious memories of her hands on other parts of his body. He couldn't stand the concern in her eyes—as if she actually cared. Averting his gaze, he caught sight of the object she threw at him. A paperweight in the shape of a baseball. Round and heavy.

Damn heavy since his cheek still throbbed with pain.

"It's starting to bruise a little. Are you okay? Maybe I should take you to the hospital."

Enough of this. He didn't want her fake concern.

Steeling his spine, he found the strength to back away from her touch. He was surprised he hadn't been able to when she'd first touched him. Her hands drifted off his cheek. And damn if it didn't piss him off that he missed her touch immediately.

"I'm fine. It doesn't hurt."

She rolled her eyes, then bent down and picked up the paperweight, setting it back on Emmett's desk. "You're a terrible liar."

Whatever. He wasn't going to admit it hurt like hell.

"What are you doing here? I'd like to know."

Her gaze narrowed on him like she was deciphering whether to continue to beat around the bush or tell him the truth. "My friend asked me to pick up some papers for her. Nothing nefarious going on. What are you doing here?"

He was going to kill Deja slowly and painfully. He didn't care that she was married to his brother, he didn't care that he lived with her brother, Dare, and they're the best of friends. None of that mattered because Deja set this up. Did she know that he and Penelope knew each other from high school? Or was she simply trying to play matchmaker?

It was, unfortunately, something she and Sophie enjoyed doing the last four months since they both tied the knot, living in married bliss. They thought he and Dare needed to be just as happy. Well, more so Deja than Sophie if he had to guess. He was about fed up with all these little tricks and games they kept playing on him and Dare. By the annoyed look Dare always gave his sister, he was sick of it as well.

"Same thing, apparently. The mysterious papers should've been on the desk out there," Ethan said with a harsh tone, pointing a hand in the direction of Deja's desk.

Oh, man, he was trying so hard to keep his cool, to hold back his anger, because he didn't get angry often. But seeing her...

Penelope...

It was too much to bear.

Penelope's eyes glanced toward the door, then back to him. "You know Deja?"

Wow. Was she that clueless? He almost thought for a moment Penelope was in on the whole ordeal because she sure liked to play games in high school.

Of course, he didn't want to think about the past.

"She's married to Emmett."

Penelope's mouth opened then closed, like a fish gulping for air. "I just moved in next door to her. I haven't met her husband yet. I had no idea."

"Well, now you know." And now he knew he wouldn't be visiting Emmett as often as long as Penelope was their neighbor.

"You're still mad at me." Her brows pleated in confusion, her eyes filling with pain. "I guess I made the right decision, then. It seems you still haven't grown up."

"Oh, I grew up. I learned not to trust certain women. The kind who loves red and says shit they don't really mean."

"That is—"

"I don't want to hear it." He shoved his hand in his pocket and pulled out his keys. "And do us both a favor and tell Deja that her little plan to get us together is a lost cause."

He slammed the office door on his way out just because he could. The sound reverberated around the tiny office.

Penelope Justice.

The only woman to ever capture his heart.

The only woman to ever destroy his heart.

Hearts and sloppy kisses...

Some people say you never forget your first love.

Well, Ethan worked hard every day to forget Penelope Justice even existed.

PENELOPE DREW in a deep breath and released it slowly in an attempt to regain her composure. She would not cry.

Damn it. She wouldn't.

Crying for the past month had been enough tears for her. Did she have any left inside? And to spill tears over that arrogant, spiteful man-child wasn't worth it. He didn't deserve her tears.

Looking around the office one more time to make sure she didn't miss the papers, she let loose a heavy sigh.

Ethan called the papers mysterious as if he knew something she didn't.

Like...

Oh no.

Deja wouldn't do that to her. Would she?

Try to set her up with some guy.

Geez, they were friendly with each other. They chatted a few times when they'd happen to be checking their mail at the same time, but she wouldn't necessarily call them friends. Like, real friends. Didn't only real friends set each other up?

Shutting off the lights, she locked the door and headed

back home to find out what was going on. When she finally pulled into her driveway less than ten minutes later, her heart was racing a mile a minute.

Gripping the steering wheel hard, she could feel her hands shaking. She took a few more deep breaths to calm herself down.

Although tears weren't on the verge this time, she could feel a panic attack threatening to surface. They didn't happen too often, but in the past month, they happened more than she cared to admit.

At first, she thought she was having a heart attack. Considering her father recently passed away from a heart attack, she didn't think it was farfetched. Except, when she visited the doctor and explained her symptoms, they said it was more than likely a panic attack, not a heart attack.

It had been so laughable she actually laughed at the doctor. Penelope Justice, all-star cheerleader, class president, and magna cum laude graduate from one of the most prestigious colleges in the country did *not* get panic attacks. Something she vehemently told the doctor. Of course, the doctor responded with a typical look she saw all the time by a few of her friends in college. The ones who always thought they were right about everything and arguing with them was pointless. She decided it wasn't worth arguing with the doctor and thanked him for his time. She also took the information about how to reduce the likelihood of a panic attack and what may be causing it.

But it was silly. Because she didn't panic. She was the calmest person in the world.

Seriously. Didn't seeing Ethan McCord, the only man to ever destroy her heart, indicate she could remain calm? Of course, she could.

She kept her composure the entire time she stood in the room with him. Even when he left, she kept her composure.

She would not allow that man to bring her down again. No, thanks. She saw the pits of hell once, and she refused to visit it again.

Breathing slowly, she let her heartbeat settle down to a comfortable pace, then relaxed her hands and removed them from the steering wheel.

No big deal. She'd have a quick chat with Deja. Let her know, in no uncertain terms, that she did not want to be set up with another guy. She was so done with dating, and she definitely didn't want to be set up with the asshole Ethan McCord.

No way. Not a chance.

As she exited her car and made her way across the lawn to Deja's front door, she knew she was lying to herself. A bad habit she had obtained in the last few weeks, if not years.

If he hadn't stormed away, she would've asked him to grab a cup of coffee or dinner—anything to have a chance to catch up, talk to him. Maybe even rekindle what they once had.

Obviously, that moment of insanity had been just that. Complete and utter insanity.

Because Ethan McCord was the same childish, irresponsible man he was at the age of eighteen when they last parted ways.

Nine years had not changed a thing.

Knocking on the door with Deja's key in her hand, she waited more impatiently than she liked. She could feel shivers wrack her body as the seconds ticked by.

The door swung open.

Luck was not on her side today.

"Wow. Oh, hey. Umm..." Emmett looked at her, confused as if grappling to remember her name.

"Penelope."

"Yeah, I knew that. I did." He smiled.

It did nothing to ease her anxiety.

Ha!

Maybe it was anxiety attacks, not panic attacks. She knew the doctor was an idiot. She did *not* have panic attacks. Although she didn't get anxious very often either. She didn't even want to say she had anxiety attacks.

There was nothing wrong with her. At all.

"Did Ethan call you?"

Emmett's eyebrows rose. "He did not. Was he supposed to? Are you two—"

"Absolutely not. He's a man-child, and I don't have time for someone like that." Penelope held out her hand. "I'm returning Deja's key. Please tell her I did not see the papers she was talking about, so I come here empty-handed besides the key."

Emmett nodded. "Right. Gotcha." He took the key from her. "Why don't I grab Deja and you two can have a chat?"

"That's not..." Her words trailed off as Emmett walked away before she could get her full sentence out.

The entire evening was turning into the worst night ever. Could it get much worse?

Deja approached the open door with an apologetic look on her face. Then a bright smile appeared as if that would butter her up or something. She only wanted to go home, pour a glass of wine, and unwind from the hectic day.

"Did your husband tell you anything?"

Deja looked surprised. Probably because of the attitude in her tone that she couldn't manage to hide. "Only that you were at the door and returning my key. He looked puzzled but didn't say anything else. Is everything okay?"

She sighed heavily. "Please tell me you didn't try to set me up with some guy. I didn't find your mysterious papers."

Sure, she mimicked Ethan's words, but it was true. Where were these papers Deja wanted?

The guilty look on Deja's face said everything.

"He's a great guy. I promise. I didn't mean any harm in it. My friend Ava is rubbing off on me because I can't stop meddling in Emmett's brother's life and my own brother." Deja widened her smile as if that would help her case. "I like you, Penelope. I think you're wonderful, and I want to see my brother-in-law Ethan with someone I like. Because I'll be honest, I'm not a fan of most of the women he dates."

Penelope lost all pretenses, not that she had much to begin with when she knocked on the door. She didn't smile. She didn't grin. She didn't give a small laugh. If anything, she gave the meanest look she owned.

"He is *not* a great guy, and he is the last man on Earth that I would ever want to be with. Trust me when I say he feels the same about me."

Wow. She just told a bald-faced lie.

She would've jumped at the chance to reunite with Ethan. She had missed him so much and...

It was better not to think about him.

"Oh." Deja winced, instantly realizing her error. "You two know each other already?"

"It was a long time ago, and I don't care to get into it. I like you, too, Deja. You've been wonderful welcoming me into the neighborhood, and I appreciate that. But please don't do this again. I'm not looking to date anyone, and if I were, it would not be Ethan McCord."

Liar!

"Got it loud and clear. I'm sorry."

Penelope couldn't deny Deja honestly looked apologetic. Therefore, she removed her angry scowl and replaced it with a smile. "How about we grab drinks later this week and forget this ever happened?"

"I would love that."

Penelope nodded and said her goodbyes. She walked calmly back across the yard to her front door when deep inside, she was aching to rush across the lawn like the devil was on her tail.

She couldn't believe she managed to unlock, open, and close her door without one shake. As soon as she was enclosed inside her sanctuary, her body started to tremble.

Deep breath in and a deep breath out.

Over and over, she did that until she was able to center herself back into reality.

What was she thinking to ask Deja to grab a drink? The woman was married to Emmett McCord. She even *lived* next to him.

If she planned to avoid the one man who could destroy her once again, she'd have to move.

Because she couldn't risk running into Ethan.

Not even once.

That composure she worked so hard to maintain would crumble into tiny shattering pieces the next time she saw him.

2

ONE LOUD RAP against the door sounded, inching up Ethan's already annoyed mood. But he couldn't ignore his brother because ignoring him wouldn't do a damn thing. If Emmett had something to say, he'd damn well say it. They all acted like that in the McCord family. It might hurt sometimes to hear the truth, but they never hid from it.

"Yo, it's open."

Ethan hated hollering it, but he preferred to get the inevitable conversation out of the way. He knew Emmett would come over after Penelope most likely told Deja what happened at the office. Which was why he left the door unlocked, knowing Emmett would stop by. And anytime he stopped over, he always rapped once on the door. It was his signature knock. His brother Gabe normally rapped twice.

He heard the door open and quietly shut, but he didn't look at his brother. He didn't even acknowledge him as he sat on the couch.

"You okay?" Emmett asked in a soft voice.

"Yep."

He didn't feel obligated to add anything else. He could

usually shake things off quickly, but seeing Penelope again after so many years... He wasn't sure how to shake it off—if he ever would.

And was he a child who needed coddling? Why did Emmet have to speak to him like he was made of glass and could shatter at any moment?

A heavy sigh escaped.

Because he'd been broken before by the same woman who cut him to pieces tonight. Just seeing her gorgeous face, her silky blonde hair that she still wore long and past her shoulders. Aww, the sweet memories of playing with her hair, being goofy and trying to braid it like he knew what the hell he was doing. It never turned out very good, but she never complained, and he enjoyed making her smile. Because she always smiled and laughed her beautiful, infectious laugh every time she looked in the mirror to see his finished product.

"He's been like that since he got home. Very quiet and in his own little world. Maybe you can tell me what's wrong with him," Dare said, who was sitting in the recliner sipping on a beer.

Dare had grabbed them beers when he got home and asked what was wrong since it must've been plastered on his face that something happened. He mumbled something— he couldn't even remember what—took the beer and sat down on the couch to watch some baseball.

He didn't want to talk about it. Not with anybody.

Emmett shifted on the couch. "Deja did her matchmaking scheme again. This time she kind of screwed up and tried to hook Ethan up with his old high school girlfriend. I'm guessing by her reaction when I saw her that it didn't go well. Did it, Ethan?"

"Well, I sure hope Deja learned her lesson to knock it

the hell off," Dare said with an irritated groan. "It's getting old."

"Hey, I have no control over your sister, and you know it." Emmett chuckled. "I've told her repeatedly to leave you two alone." Emmett nudged Ethan's thigh softly with his fist. "She promised she wouldn't do it again. And she's sorry if she opened any old wounds. Seriously, man, you okay?"

He turned to his brother, unable to hide the pain in his eyes. "She's as beautiful as the day she left. I wasn't too pleasant with her. She hates my guts."

Emmett didn't hide his wince, which told Ethan everything he needed to know. She hated his guts. And why wouldn't she after his parting words?

"I need another beer. You want one?"

Before he could stand up, Emmett touched his shoulder to keep him sitting. "Drowning your sorrows isn't going to help. Sound familiar?"

Oh, yeah, it sure did. He said the same exact thing to Emmett when he was going through issues with Deja. But damn, he understood now. It might not help, but it would dull the pain for a while.

"Work has been crazy, and I didn't know she was the one who moved in next to us. Deja told me some things Penelope told her. She moved in about a month ago. She used to live in New York, but she moved back to be closer to her family." Emmett frowned. "Her dad passed away about two weeks ago. He suffered a heart attack. So much for moving to be closer to her family."

His head fell back against the couch as he closed his eyes. He had no idea her dad died—and so recently. Maybe some of his friends knew, but they also knew he didn't like to talk about Penelope or hear things about her. Maybe that's why nobody told him. She and her dad had been close growing up. He even tried to use her tight-knit relationship with her father as an excuse for her to stay. She still left anyway. No reason, no argument he ever made, had been enough to keep her here.

"That's rough," Dare said quietly.

"Yeah, it is." Emmett tapped him on the shoulder this time, waiting until he popped his head up and looked at him. "What do you want?"

He eyed his brother quizzically. "What do you mean?"

Emmett arched a brow like he was the biggest idiot on the planet. "You know what I mean. She called you a man-child. I can't disagree with her at the moment."

"Go to hell, man. Get out. I'm done talking." Ethan stood up, finished listening to this shit. He'd grab another beer like he originally wanted to.

Emmett rose as well, grabbing him by the front of the shirt to prevent him from walking away. "You were a mess when she left. Gabe and I helped you through it. You moved on, you forgot about her, and now you date every woman who walks by you."

Ethan shoved him off and gave a cruel laugh. "Yeah, but I don't sleep with every single one of them. There's nothing wrong with having some fun. Half of those women are my friends."

"You didn't let me finish," Emmett said, crossing his arms as if he needed an extra barrier to prevent himself from grabbing his shirt again. Ethan wasn't opposed to hitting his brother, not with the anxious, angry energy flowing through his veins.

Where was this intense anger coming from? He never yelled at his brothers like this.

"Go ahead, finish your asinine speaking."

Emmett chuckled, glancing behind him to Dare. "How

do you live with him? Does he always act like a petulant child?"

Dare chuckled but remained silent otherwise. Very wise man. Ethan was so close to losing his patience.

"One short interaction with her and look at how you're acting."

"What about it?" Ethan shot back. "I wasn't prepared to see her again. Hell, I didn't want to see her ever again. So tell your wife I'm pissed at her."

"Are you pissed at Deja? Or are you pissed at yourself because you let her get away?"

Ethan's mouth dropped open in shock. "Let her get away? She left. She broke it off and told me it was over not even a week after she'd told me she loved me and couldn't wait to spend the rest of her life with me. She's nothing but a damn liar. If she'd really loved me, she never would've left."

Emmett's arms dropped to his sides. "And if you had loved her, you would've understood why she wanted to go to college somewhere else. She wanted to spread her wings, learn new things, enjoy a new way of life, which I might add is part of growing up and finding yourself. The way I understood it was, she didn't want to lose you, even though she was moving away for college. But your thick head never wanted to see it that way. You're an idiot, man."

Ethan shook his head, knowing he wasn't the idiot. His brother was. He had no idea what he was talking about. She left. She told him she never wanted to see him again the last time they saw each other before she headed off to college. Oh, he understood her perfectly clear. She took his love and destroyed it with false hope.

She never loved him. Not like he had loved her.

Had?

Hell, he still loved her. He never stopped. Which was why he always dated casually and never too serious. He didn't want to love anyone else. She had been his one and only, even if he couldn't spend the rest of his life with her.

"Apologize to her. Ask her out. I know you still love her," Emmett said.

So his brother was a damn mind reader now? Of course, maybe his love for her was written all over his face. But that sure as hell didn't mean he was going to admit it out loud, not even to his brother. And especially not to her.

"Hey, Emmett. Get the hell out of my house."

Then he turned around and stalked out of the room before anyone could stop him. He even slammed his bedroom door for extra measure, then locked it in case his brother didn't get the hint.

Yeah, so he was acting like a spoiled child not getting his way.

Whatever.

His brother didn't understand how he felt. How seeing her again had whisked him back to the day she broke his heart and stomped all over it like she wanted to make sure each shard disintegrated into a tiny million pieces.

HE COULD SEE the tremble in her hand, but he was confused since it wasn't going to be the first time they had sex. They had it as often as they could, which wasn't an easy feat still living at home with their parents. But luck was on their side today because his parents were out for the evening, and his brothers were hanging out with friends. They had the house to themselves. Just one more month and school would be done; they'd be graduates and free to move out and move in together. Then they wouldn't have to worry about things like this.

So why was she nervous?

"Hey, come here," Ethan said softly, grabbing her hand and pulling her closer. He could even feel a slight tremble in her body. Running a slow, sensual hand down her back, he smiled. "What's wrong? Did you fail Mr. Pazely's math test? I'm sure most of us failed it. That shit was hard."

A tiny smile appeared, working to alleviate some of his anxiety. He always loved seeing her smile. He did anything and everything in his power to produce a smile anytime he needed a small dose of it.

"We need to talk."

He pressed a light kiss to her lips, needing something to soothe his rattled nerves. He hated how she'd said those four simple words. "We are talking."

She brought her hands up to his chest and pressed them over his heart. "I got accepted."

"Okay. That's cool." He had no idea what she was talking about.

Her brows drooped low. "You didn't apply like you said you would, did you?"

Oh, she was talking about that. Applying for college. His hands slightly loosened from around her slim body. Her hands instinctively pressed harder.

"I don't want to move that far away. New York is too far." Not to mention he wasn't smart enough for the school she wanted to attend. He was barely getting passing grades as it was, and going to some prestigious school out east wouldn't be easy for him.

"It sounds like your cousin, Jimmy, might move there, too, when he graduates. You'll have family there. I won't, but at least we'll be together."

Yeah, but the difference between him and his cousin was

Jimmy wanted to move there. He had no desire to live in a big city, surrounded by millions of people. Of course, he planned to go to school and everything, but he wanted to stick around locally. He'd apply for a school that he knew he could handle. Moving out east sounded like too much pressure he didn't want. He aspired to be a firefighter one day. He didn't need to go to some fancy school for that. He wanted to help people, protect them, and be by his family. He couldn't do the last part if he was thousands of miles away from home. And protecting his family was important to him. His cousins lost their mom when they were kids. Although she didn't die from a fire, the fire that hit their farm didn't help her health issues. If only the firefighters would've stopped the fire sooner before it destroyed the entire barn and filled the surrounding area with so much smoke, maybe his cousins' mom might've had a few more months—or even a year—to live.

Since the day the devastating fire destroyed half the farm, the death of his cousins' mom—he knew then he wanted to help people.

"No, we won't, Penelope." He shook his head. "You're right. I didn't apply. I don't want to go to school there. What about your dad? What does he think? You won't have family there, and you're close with your dad."

"He understands. He wants the best for me. I'll miss him, but he'll visit me, and I'll visit him. It's not forever."

Was she implying he didn't want the best for her? Because he did. He did, damn it. But he didn't want to see her moving so far away.

She swallowed hard, the trembles in her hands intensifying. "And us?"

"What about us?"

She squeezed her fists into tight balls, scrunching his shirt, then shoved away from him. "Are you obtuse, or are you trying to ignore the problem?"

"What problem? You don't need to go to college so far away."

Her bottom lip quivered, then stopped. "But I want to, Ethan."

He looked away, hating the sadness in her eyes—hating that the conversation was derailing into a territory he didn't want to visit. Okay, yeah, he was trying to ignore the problem. He didn't want to lose her.

"Fine, whatever. Go." But he already lost her. She got accepted into the college she wanted, and she was leaving, even though she said she loved him and would always be with him. Apparently, love wasn't enough for her. She was leaving him.

"Go?"

His gaze whipped to hers. "Yeah, go. If that's what you want, just go."

"I don't even know what you mean by 'go.' Go to New York? Go away? Go home? Go and don't come back? Why can't we talk this out like two rational adults?"

"What's there to talk about? I'm not going, you want to go." He shrugged, confused about what more they could say to each other.

She was leaving him. He definitely didn't want to talk about that.

Walking to her backpack sitting on the floor near his bed, she picked it up and slung it over her shoulder.

"It's impossible to have a real conversation with you. When you're ready to talk about this, then come talk to me. Otherwise, I guess I'll never see you again."

Then she walked out of his room and out of his life.

3

Hunching her shoulders, wishing she would've grabbed her hoodie like she originally planned, she tried to meld into the background. Not that one could hide very well standing in front of a bin of bright ripe oranges.

Before she could whisk her cart in the opposite direction and hightail it out of the store, Ethan caught sight of her.

They stared at each other like two deer in headlights.

She had been back over a month and not once did she run into him. Since she saw him two days ago, she'd seen him a few times in town, not that he ever noticed her. This was the first time they'd officially made eye contact.

Honestly, she swore he would've caught her gawking when she saw him yesterday outside the fire station doing what she assumed was drills of some sort. He hadn't been shirtless or anything—something she would've loved to see. He had been dressed in full turnout gear, and although covered from head to toe in what she could only imagine was heavy clothing, he'd been sexy as hell. Of course, any man in that kind of uniform was sexy; she had no problem admitting that. Not that she'd admit it to Ethan.

A fire truck had been sitting outside the station with the ladder raised. She had watched while he climbed the ladder, doing a few other things she found fascinating, completely mesmerized by his fearlessness. Did he do that during an actual fire—climb close to the flames and save people? She couldn't picture it.

Because the guy she remembered loved to make jokes and goof around, skip class because it was a nice day out. He didn't do brave, scary things like climb a ladder several stories high amid scalding heat.

She flinched when another guy approached Ethan's cart and tossed a box inside. She didn't pay attention to the contents; her eyes were glued to Ethan.

"I thought about hanging over by the kiwi and strawberries a little bit longer, but I wasn't sure how long you two were going to keep staring at each other. So, here I am." The man then stepped closer to her and held out his hand. "Hi, I'm Dare, Deja's brother. You must be Penelope because I've never seen Ethan speechless in front of a woman before."

Dumbfounded, but not wanting to be rude since he was Deja's brother, she shook his hand. "It's nice to meet you. Deja's been very kind to me, welcoming me to the neighborhood."

"Yeah, real kind," Ethan muttered.

Dare glanced at him, then back to her. She didn't miss the warning glare Dare gave him. "Well, uh, it was nice meeting you. I guess we'll keep shopping and let you do the same."

"Of course. You have a wonderful evening, Dare." Then she flashed Ethan a bright smile, refusing to let him get the last word in this time. "You can continue to rot in hell."

She plucked two oranges from the bin, set them in her cart, and walked away, feeling triumph in the way Ethan drew back in surprise. If he wanted to say mean, cruel things to her, then she could play that game, too.

Her heart dipped.

Not that she wanted to.

She finished the rest of her shopping as quickly as possible, forgoing a few things on her list because she didn't want to run into Ethan again. Purchasing her things with frantic glances to the cashier to speed it up, she rushed to her car like she was on a game show.

She threw her bags into the trunk without even taking care to not crush the eggs, shoved her cart in the corral and quickly jumped into the driver's seat.

Before she could start the key, her heart started to race, her vision blurring.

"Oh, no. Not now. Keep calm. Just keep calm."

She gripped the steering wheel, her hands trembling. Closing her eyes, she tried to focus on her breathing.

In and out.

In and out.

Then a rush of air hit her as her door swung open.

"Penelope... Hey, it's okay." Ethan's warm hand touched her cheek, forcing her to turn her head. "Look at me."

Her eyes popped open.

"That's right. Slow, even breaths. It's okay."

She listened to his soothing voice as he instructed her to keep breathing in and out. Her heartbeat took its time to settle at a normal pace. Her panicked and chaotic breathing began to calm, finally finding its rhythm.

"You're okay."

But was she?

The man she loved, the man she would always love, hated her. He might be showing kindness right now, but he hated her. He wanted absolutely nothing to do with her.

For the first time, his expression softened, reminding her of the old days when they were young and in love.

"Move over. I'll drive you home." His hand dropped from her cheek.

"I'm fine."

His eyes glittered with...desire? "I'll pick you up and deposit you in the passenger seat if I have to, but I'm driving you home."

Her hands, still gripping the steering wheel, continued to tremble. Maybe her breathing was back to normal, but he was right. She shouldn't drive herself home.

Scooting across the console to the passenger seat, she buckled her seat belt and wondered if she was giving in so easily just to spend more time with him.

Probably.

"What about your groceries?"

Ethan closed the door and started the same car she bought with her hard-earned money when she was sixteen years old.

"Dare will take care of it. It's fine." He backed out of the parking spot, flashing her a brief smile. "I can't believe you still have this car."

She ran a hand over the dashboard. "You better not say anything bad about my baby. She still runs smooth as butter. Got me to New York and back again."

Sudden tension filled the car.

Now, who was the idiot? Her.

Why did she have to mention New York?

"I guess we'll call her Old Red, instead of just Red." A low chuckle floated out of his lips.

Turning her attention in his direction, she couldn't help but laugh with him. She had always been a fan of red. Red shoes, red lipstick, red dresses, red anything. So, of course, when she shopped for a car, it had to be red. Ethan, the jokester he loved to be, dubbed her car Red. Not very original, but when he used to tease her about it in his tender, adoring way, she loved it.

"She might be old, but she's a pure jewel. Never lets me down."

Ugh. More slimy, icky tension filled the car.

Why did she keep saying things that were itching to create another battle between them?

Ethan turned on the radio, and the rest of the drive was made in silence besides the sweet country tunes filling the car.

When he pulled into her driveway, less than fifteen minutes later, she tried to think of the best way to say thank you. She knew he hated her—he didn't have to show her this level of kindness.

Then Ethan flashed her another brief smile. "I'll help you bring in the groceries."

Before she could argue, he was opening the door and sliding out of the vehicle with her keys in his hand.

He popped the trunk and started to grab half of the bags. Unless she wanted to look like an ungrateful bitch, she needed to grab the other half and follow him, which she did, but she did so begrudgingly...and confused.

Why was he suddenly being so nice?

Pity?

Great. Most likely. He saw her in a moment of weakness, and now he felt sorry for her.

As if he did this often, he carried all the groceries at once, unlocking the door at the same time, swiftly making entry and heading to the left like he'd been there before.

She followed him, curious if he had. She had purchased the house from an older couple, but they did have a daughter close to her age. Had Ethan hooked up with her?

Not her concern. She didn't care who he had dated in the past. Or who he planned to date in the future. She. Did. Not. Care.

Plunking the bags down on the counter, way more ungracefully than he had, she turned to him with a smile. A very forced, very fake smile. She was afraid she was about to lose her composure once again.

"Thanks. I appreciate it."

"Not a problem." Then he started opening the bags and pulling things out.

Not a problem? There was nothing but problems between them. And why was he suddenly putting her groceries away?

"What are you doing?"

He paused as he put a can of diced tomatoes in the pantry. "It's not obvious?"

Well, of course, it was obvious what he was physically doing, but why? "You don't have to help me put the groceries away. I can handle it."

He flashed her a silky smile, a hint of irritation laced behind it. "I know you're very capable of a lot of things."

Oh, that could mean so many things. Was he gearing for a fight? Fighting was the last thing she wanted. Actually, all she wanted was for him to leave so she could break down in peace.

Except she didn't do anything but watch him as he unloaded bag after bag, searching for where all the items went and producing a triumphant smile when he found the right location.

She should help. She should say thank you. And she definitely shouldn't act like such a bitch, but she couldn't help it. His ulterior motive was unknown, and that's what stopped her from moving a muscle. He had to have an ulterior motive. Why was he being so nice?

The crinkling noise from all the bags as he scrunched them together when he finished putting the last item away filled the tiny kitchen. "Do you save the bags?"

Pointing to the pantry, she nodded. "There's a pretty flower bag hanging to the side that my grandma made."

Another adorable smile etched across his face before he turned toward the pantry and tucked all the bags away where they belonged.

"There. All done. That wasn't too hard," he said as he twisted back in her direction.

"You can leave now." She winced and closed her eyes at how rude that came out. That was not what she meant to say. A simple thank you would've been much better. Or even —don't ever leave.

A warm hand caressed her cheek.

Her eyes slowly opened.

"And if I don't want to leave...?"

Her brows shot up in surprise. What game was he playing now?

Then his other hand gripped the side of her hip.

Oh, she didn't care what game he was playing. For over nine years, she imagined his hands on her body, doing things they had never ventured into as teenagers. She wouldn't say she never indulged with other men or tried to date and find a man she could marry because she did.

But Ethan never left her mind. He invaded her senses, her soul like a demon taking control.

"This is a bad idea, Ethan," she whispered softly. She didn't want to say it at all, but one of them had to.

"Oh, it definitely is. But I need you so badly, I don't know how to stop myself."

Then his lips were on hers, tasting, tempting, and devouring her like he was a starving man.

She let him because she didn't want to stop herself... or him.

ETHAN COULDN'T SUPPRESS a delightful groan as he dropped his hand from her cheek and pulled her closer.

This was worse than a bad idea, but he honestly couldn't stop himself. The longer they tangled tongues, the more he knew he wouldn't be able to stop unless she pushed him away.

He had been speechless in the store when they saw each other. Then he became irritated when Dare walked up and said something first. Although what he would've said to her, he had no idea.

He had two long days to think about the things Emmett said. That maybe he had twisted the argument they had years ago to his way of thinking. He didn't want her to leave. She wanted to go. Not once did she ever say she wanted to break up, but how would they've ever made a long-distance relationship work?

Seeing her again after so many years, missing her, craving her, thinking about her when he didn't want to—it brought back those painful memories of losing her. That's why he acted like an asshole.

He had been all prepared in the store to apologize for his behavior, but no words would come out. Then Dare stepped in, and he lost his chance.

An erotic moan slipped from her lips.

His hands brushed down her back and cupped her ass, and just like old times, she quickly caught on to his hinting, jumping into his arms and wrapping her legs around his waist.

The kiss deepened as his grip tightened on her body.

God, he missed this. Holding her, kissing her, feeling her in his arms.

He had walked around the store, trying to seek her out, ignoring Dare as he spoke about a bunch of nonsense. He probably thought he was helping him out by trying to distract him. He had to nudge Dare to the checkout line when he finally spotted her paying for her things. She started walking out of the store before they were finished.

He knew his chances were gone if he didn't stop her and tell her how sorry he was for acting like a jackass.

Then he saw her sitting in her car. He recognized the signs immediately. Working as a firefighter, he saw too many harrowing things over the course of his career. People in a panic. People acting crazy because they didn't know how to rein in their terror. People crying or shouting in anger and fear. People standing as still as a statue because they were in so much shock.

Yeah, he'd seen it all.

And it nearly broke him when he saw Penelope struggling with herself. All because of him.

He was worse than a jackass, making her feel that unsettled.

That jarred him out of his bliss. He needed to apologize. Then maybe they could have what they once had. The entire time he put the groceries away, he tried to find the right words, but none came. Now was the time to get an apology out.

His lips broke away, his breathing heavy, his grip tight on her.

"Penelope—"

"Down the hall and on the right." Her eyes glittered with desire.

Oh.

Okay.

She wanted to go that far. More than a simple kiss. Not that there had been anything simple about the kiss they shared.

But he needed to apologize first. He started to open his mouth when her lips connected with his.

So, she didn't want to talk. Yeah, talking was overrated, anyway.

He turned around and started leaving a trail of kisses across her neck as he followed her instructions to her bedroom. Once there, he lay her on the bed and started removing her clothes.

He felt like he was whisked back in time—back when he was a bumbling teenager, about to have sex for the first time. In a way, it was just like that. It had been nine years since he last had Penelope in his arms and he wanted it to be perfect. Exactly like their first time had been. Well, as perfect as it could be between two virgins.

He tossed her shirt behind him, taking his time to unclasp her bra. It was one of those fun ones with the clasp in the front—her breasts spilling out like they were wanting to be free, aching for his touch. Oh, and he didn't hesitate to caress and nibble before removing the bra completely and moving to unhook the button on her pants, taking them off as well. Penelope kept her eyes on him the entire time—her gaze lit up with pleasure.

Tossing off his shirt, then kicking off his shoes and

sliding his jeans and boxers down, he stopped to grab a condom from his wallet.

"You forgot about my panties," she said with a wicked smile.

"I have to do everything around here?" he asked with his own devilish smile. He grabbed his cock and pumped his hand once, her eyes following the movement.

"Yes, you do."

Setting the condom on the bed, he hovered above her, his mouth inches from hers. "If you insist, sweetheart."

A beautiful smile appeared. A smile he had been dying to see for years—not just in his dreams.

He kissed her before slowly trailing his tongue down her body, his mouth closing over her nipple. He teased, nipped and tugged until a low, throaty moan left her delectable lips. Wanting the torturous pleasure to last as long as possible, he kissed and licked a path down her slender body until he reached the top of her black lace panties. He gripped the fabric between his teeth, pulling them down until the most private part of her body was exposed. He placed a kiss on her most sensitive spot—something he'd never done when they were teenagers.

But they weren't kids anymore. No longer were they two inexperienced eighteen-year-olds who knew nothing about pleasuring each other.

He sucked, tasted, devoured her as if she were the sweetest treat he'd ever had, and he didn't stop until a low cry of bliss escaped her lips. Her hands delved into his hair and pulled hard. He almost cried out in pain, but he'd take it in silence, knowing it was a result of her pleasure.

And they weren't finished.

He slid her panties down the rest of the way and

grabbed the condom, pumping his cock a few times before putting it on.

"Ethan..." His name left her mouth in a tender whisper.

Centering himself over her, he paused before entering. "Yes, Penelope?"

Her eyes captured his.

"Nothing to say?"

A smile appeared, but no words left her mouth.

He chuckled, loving the fact he'd rendered her speechless. It seemed only fair since she had done the same thing to him at the store. And hell, they'd only been looking at each other.

He slowly entered her, taking his time to relish in the glorious bliss. Oh, man, he didn't remember it feeling this delicious being inside her. She felt like she was made for him.

How in the hell had he survived nine years without her?

He started to slowly thrust, savoring the moment, but Penelope must've decided that wasn't enough for her. She wrapped her legs around his waist and dug her heels into his ass, urging him to move faster. He happily obliged; he'd never been able to resist giving Penelope whatever she wanted.

Except for his support when she wanted to go to college away from their hometown.

Not something he wanted to think about right now. He still needed to apologize for his behavior.

Ignoring his damaging thoughts, he pumped harder, thrusting in and out with complete abandon. Penelope held on and enjoyed the ride as he went wild with pleasure.

Before he could stop, prolong it some more, his orgasm hit. He groaned, stiffened, and let it flow through him. Such glorious ecstasy.

Placing a few tender kisses on her neck, he then kissed her lips before meeting her gaze.

"Damn, sweetheart." Another kiss touched her lips because he wanted to ignore what he just said. Those weren't the elegant words he meant to say.

Then he rolled off her and stood up. "I'll be right back."

She eyed him funny. "Where are you going?"

"To the bathroom. To throw away the condom." Where else would he go? What an odd question.

He quickly disposed of the condom, washed his hands, and walked back to her bedroom. He jerked back in surprise and couldn't hide his shocked expression when he found her fully dressed and standing next to the bed. His clothes were neatly folded on the edge of the bed.

"Not a cuddler, then?" he asked with a laugh, attempting to hide how disappointed he was.

"You know your way around this house very well."

"Umm...yeah."

The pleasure and passion they experienced were gone from her eyes. A deep frown punctured her beautiful face.

"What's going on here, Penelope? Did I do something wrong in the span of ten seconds?"

"This wasn't simply a bad idea..." She drew in a deep breath and continued, "...it was a mistake."

Ouch!

That hurt.

That hurt more than her leaving nine years ago.

He was a mistake.

So much for apologizing. He was nothing but a good lay to her.

Or, hell, maybe she didn't think he was that good. He got her off with his tongue, but he didn't with his dick.

"A mistake?"

"I'm sorry, Ethan. I—"

"Yep. Me, too. I meant to say that before we slept together, but I'll get it out of the way now. Sorry for being a jackass nine years ago. I guess I was too late in that regard because I'm still a mistake."

Her eyes narrowed as the anger flared to life. "Well, I'm apparently just another woman in the long line of women you have. Yay me."

"Excuse me?"

Now he was lost in the conversation.

"You know the layout of the house."

"Yeah, I think we already established that."

"Because you dated the previous owner's daughter." A tired smile twisted her lips. "I'm simply another woman on the notch of your bedpost."

This time his expression hardened in anger.

"No, Penelope. I never did. I know the layout of the house because it's the same layout as Emmett's. All the damn houses are the same around here."

He swiped his clothes from the bed and his shoes from the floor and stalked out of the room.

So much for thinking they could rekindle what they once had.

She thought he was a womanizing player.

4

———

PENELOPE GRABBED her soft down blanket closer to her chest, snuggling under the warmth, and brought her glass full of wine closer to her lips.

She held the drink close to her mouth since she had the blanket wrapped all around her, so it wasn't too hard to keep taking sip after sip after sip.

As fast as she was going, she'd have the whole bottle polished off sooner rather than later.

What an idiot!

First, she calls that beautiful moment between them a mistake—it was *so* not a mistake. It had been everything and more. Way more than her late-night dreams and daytime musings could ever replicate.

How had she lived so far away from him for nine long years?

Why had she ruined the moment?

Because then, of course, she had to make it worse and accuse him of being a player. It had seemed plausible he dated the woman. He knew the house so well. It was just...odd. Although she didn't know his dating status, how often he dated, what kind of women he dated, whether he had been married and divorced, or close to marriage. But back in high school, before they started dating in tenth grade, he had been smooth with the ladies.

He had definitely been smooth with her when he ran into her coming out of the boys' locker room and knocked all her books out of her hand. He had picked everything up, apologized, smiled in that wicked way she loved, and asked her to the homecoming dance as if it weren't a big deal.

And it had been a huge deal because that was the first time they had ever spoken more than two words together. The oh-so-popular Ethan McCord never even looked in her direction. All-star baseball champion. Every girl's dream guy. The favorite student for all the teachers—but only because he was such a smooth talker—his grades were never that great.

Ethan McCord...

She slept with Ethan McCord.

She loved Ethan McCord.

She ruined her chances of ever having a relationship with the one and only Ethan McCord.

Taking another sip of wine, she jumped, making wine slosh over the rim when a knock sounded on her door.

About an hour had passed since Ethan left.

Had he come back?

Pushing the blanket off and setting the glass on the coffee table, she wiped away the little wine that dripped on her hand as she walked to the door.

Peeking through the peephole, needing to be completely prepared for another standoff with Ethan, her brow lifted at who stood on the other side.

She opened the door and offered a forced smile. "Hi, Deja."

"Hey, I hope I'm not bothering you at a bad time or anything."

"Of course not. Come in." She stepped aside to let Deja enter, wondering if she knew Ethan had stopped over.

Was she fishing for information?

"What's up?"

Deja inhaled deeply, then let it out slowly.

Oh, boy.

Like she was preparing to say something she wouldn't like.

"You asked if we could have drinks later this week."

Her heart started to pound.

Oh, no.

Not now.

Not a panic attack.

Ethan must've said something to her, told her to leave her alone, and now Deja didn't want anything to do with her.

"Are you okay, Penelope?" Deja started to reach out toward her.

She took a step back, forcing herself to relax, but it didn't work as her heart rate continued to speed up.

"I'm fine. You should leave."

Deja's blue eyes sparkled with defiance.

Odd.

"You don't look okay right now, and if you're still upset about what I did the other day, I apologize. I swear I won't do it again. I just wanted to ask if you wanted to join me and my friends for a drink later tonight. In about a half hour, actually. I'm meeting my friends Sophie and Ava. That was all."

Oh, now she felt like a fool.

Her hands slightly shook, and her heart still pounded, but she could feel the tension in her body start to relax.

Talk about overreacting.

"Oh, of course. I'd like that."

"Yeah, you want to join us? That would be great." Deja grinned brightly as if she truly meant it.

It had been so long since she had a real friend. She got along fine with most of the people she went to college with, but she never connected on a deeper level where they talked about personal things. Like confessing about Ethan. She never told a soul she left the love of her life back at home.

Since moving back home, she had yet to reconnect with any of her high school friends. She wasn't sure why.

Maybe because she didn't want to get into any kind of conversation about Ethan McCord.

Deja was married to his brother.

It wouldn't be wise to go out with her.

"I think—"

"We'll drive together. I'll come back in about thirty minutes. Okay?" Deja's voice brokered no argument.

"Okay."

One time. She would go out to drinks with her one time only.

Deja left, and she got ready. Thirty minutes wasn't enough time for her to take a shower, so she changed clothes, trying hard not to look at her bed that reminded her of Ethan. She freshened up her makeup, combed her hair, then grabbed her purse right as another knock sounded on her door.

Deja was prompt. Very nice. Penelope was as well and hated waiting for anything. When she first started dating Ethan, she couldn't count how many times she had to wait for him to pick her up or get off baseball practice. So many times he would decide to stay to run a few extra plays with some of the other guys.

After three years of dating, Ethan became very smart with what ticked her off and what made her happy. He had learned not to be late picking her up. Ever. Well, baseball practice had always been a losing battle because he loved the sport too much. Any other reason she would get irritated with him for being late.

She called it a compromise.

They made idle chitchat on the way to Chico's Bar and Grill, a place she hadn't tried yet since being back. It was recently built and hadn't been around when she lived here as a teenager.

Sadly, she hadn't ventured out of her house much since moving back. The most she ever did was visit her dad, and now that he was gone, leaving the house was even rarer.

One day soon she'd have to get her shit together, woman up and find a job. She couldn't survive forever on the tiny savings she'd built up over the years. Because her dad had saved up as well, he managed to pay for her college. She didn't have that worry over her head. It might've helped that her mother had also left her a trust fund before she'd died when Penelope was a little girl. So, money wasn't an issue. But she couldn't stay locked inside her home, afraid to meet the world head-on. That's not who she was.

But she didn't want to think about that right now.

Deja walked into the bar first, waved at two women waiting at a high-top table, then introduced her.

She knew this would be a night from hell as soon as she told them who they were.

Ava McCord. Wife to Zane McCord, cousin to Ethan.

Sophie McCord. Wife to Austin McCord, cousin to Ethan.

She was at a table surrounded by McCord women.

"Deja tells us you went to college in New York and recently moved back. I'm a born-and-bred New Yorker myself. How did you like living there?" Ava asked, the excitement in her eyes to talk to someone who lived in the Big Apple.

"It was simply wonderful." Until the end. Then it was nothing but a nightmare.

She didn't want to talk about New York, so she hoped keeping her answers short would give her a clue.

"I miss it, but it does hold some painful memories. Losing Jimmy was the worst." Ava offered a smile as the pain reflected in her eyes. "That would be my husband's brother. He was a good friend of mine in the police department. He died in the line of duty."

The bottom of her stomach dropped to the floor.

One, because Deja never spilled the beans who she truly was to these women. That she had a prior relationship with Ethan. And she couldn't have been more grateful.

Two, because she had no idea Jimmy had passed away. Such a wonderful, sweet guy who didn't deserve to die so young. Her dad never told her, and he always kept her up-to-date with what was going on in town.

"Are you okay, Penelope?" Sophie asked in a soft voice.

That was the second time in an hour someone had asked her that.

No. No, she didn't think she was okay at all.

"I knew Jimmy. That's terrible news." Her words came out in a whisper.

"Oh, I had no idea. I guess if you lived here before you went to college that would make sense. I wasn't thinking." Ava's expression morphed into a brutal pain, almost a shared pain as if she were reliving the news of his death with her. "I call it having a mom-brain. I swear I'm losing my mind half the time. And little Jimmy is going on eight months. I don't want to know how I'm going to act when he's a teenager."

She produced a tiny smile. Ava was trying to loosen her tension, and it was working. "He sounds delightful."

"Oh, he's the most precious thing in the world." Ava pulled out her phone and showed her a few pictures.

She saw the McCord resemblance immediately. A very handsome baby who would grow up to be as handsome as the other men in the family.

"I didn't mean to bring the mood down. Some days I think of him and I can't help myself," Ava said morosely, the regret in her eyes. "But I find talking about him helps. Most of the time, anyway."

Penelope wasn't sure why Ava felt the need to explain herself, especially when her facial expression said she wanted to cry a bucket of tears.

"I just slept with Ethan McCord and screwed it up colossally."

The words popped out of her mouth without thinking anything through.

Deja spewed her beer as she had been taking a sip. Sophie looked at her wide-eyed. And Ava tilted her head, her brows puckered in confusion.

Then Ava stood up with a devilish smile twisting her lips, the pain in her eyes slowly dissipating. "This story sounds like it calls for a round of shots."

ETHAN ROTATED HIS NECK, trying to get the kinks free, then stepped out of the shower. The nice, hot shower did nothing to erase the memory of Penelope wrapped in his arms.

But he had to try to wipe away the memories somehow. He'd never survive otherwise.

Hell, he wasn't sure how he would regardless.

Nine long years he'd lived without her.

The moment she popped back in his life, he acted like a jackass. Somehow, they moved past that, slept together and had the most amazing sex...and then...

She called him a mistake.

Wow.

Yeah, maybe it was a mistake.

Because his heart was torn and mangled to pieces more than it ever was in the past.

Maybe this was her way of getting back at him for treating her so poorly a few days ago. Of course, Penelope wasn't a vindictive person. He couldn't imagine it.

Yet, she called him a mistake.

Getting dressed in one of the fire station's T-shirts and a pair of old, faded blue jeans, he walked barefoot to the kitchen and grabbed a beer. He should just grab two right off the bat. Or maybe he should start his shift early. He had to work tomorrow, but he wouldn't mind going in right now to get his mind off of Penelope.

Or he could grab two beers and erase his mind that way.

Drowning your sorrows isn't going to help.

His brother's voice penetrated his thoughts. His own words thrown in his face.

He settled for one, knowing getting piss-ass drunk wouldn't make the reality of Penelope thinking he was a mistake go away. Plus, he could still go into work early if he only had one. But he needed something *now* to drown out his damn sorrows.

Maybe she even thought dating him in high school had been a mistake. Perhaps that's why she left so easily and without fighting for them.

He slumped down on the couch.

What was he thinking? He didn't fight much either. Not even one word.

Stop.

Or two words.

Don't go.

Or even four words.

I love you, always.

Glancing around the quiet living room, he wondered where Dare went. He saw the groceries they purchased were stocked and put away. His truck was in the driveway. Considering he didn't want to respond to any inquiries about what happened between him and Penelope, he had walked home from her house. It didn't take too long. About twenty minutes. Which was one reason he took a shower.

The door suddenly swung open, and Dare walked in, nodding and smiling at him, then closed the door.

"How'd everything go?"

He took a sip of beer before responding. "Fine."

Dare rolled his eyes, chuckling. "Which translates into not fine. Whatever, dude. If you don't want to talk about it, it's cool."

Ethan nodded once, grateful Dare understood he didn't want to talk. They had an easygoing friendship.

Dare walked out of the living room.

He didn't know why when he first met Dare he offered a room to him, but it felt right. Although it was rocky at the start, especially with the tension between Emmett and Deja, they got along well. Like they had been the best of friends forever.

Ethan would do anything for Dare, and vice versa. He knew it without asking that Dare would be there for him. He'd had a rough life. Spending ten years behind bars had changed Dare from a troubled teenager into a hardened man. Sometimes Dare struggled with the outside world, and Ethan, as his best friend and roommate, always did his best to help him along.

Dare came back in with his own beer and took a seat on the recliner. He normally chilled out on the couch, while Dare relaxed in the recliner. Most nights, they hung out when he wasn't at work and after Dare finished working. Sometimes working 24-hour shifts at the fire station sucked because he enjoyed hanging out with Dare and being away for twenty-four hours at a time could be rough. It could be hell on his social life at times. Other times he loved being at the station surrounded by what he considered his "other family." He'd do anything for the guys he worked with.

And he'd do anything for Dare.

On weekends they ventured out for a few drinks, picking up women, or at least chatting them up. It was funny Penelope thought he was a player. Because in reality, although he flirted relentlessly with women, he rarely dated. He liked to make women smile and feel good, and a little light flirting never hurt.

But dating...

His heart usually couldn't handle it. The few relationships he had were light and carefree. Nothing ever too heavy. As soon as he had a weird inkling they were falling in love, he broke it off.

He'd only ever loved one woman.

Penelope Justice.

Even though he couldn't have her, he didn't think his heart had room to love another. So he didn't even try.

Dare, when they went out, was always too nervous and shy to talk to women. Not that he displayed an ounce of shyness, but deep down, Ethan knew he was a bundle of nerves. Because he didn't think he was good enough.

What woman wanted to date a felon?

Dare had said that quite a few times. Being a light-hearted jokester, usually to lighten the mood, he'd crack a joke or change the conversation. He'd do anything to make sure Dare never fell down the rabbit hole.

"What should we watch?" Dare asked as he grabbed the remote.

Ethan wished he had it in him right now to lighten the mood somehow. But he didn't know what to say. He didn't have anything to laugh about.

"Why don't we go out for a drink? Pick up some women."

That wasn't exactly what he meant to say. He definitely didn't want to bring a random woman home either.

But hey, Dare needed to break out of his shell. He was doing it for him. And it was either find a good woman for Dare or head into work early.

Dare cocked a brow, seeing right through him. He knew it by the intensity of his stare.

Before Dare could respond, two taps sounded on the door.

"Yo, come in."

His brother Gabe stepped inside and closed the door before taking a seat next to him.

By the light shade of red shading his cheeks, he knew what he was here for.

It was his turn to make him feel better about Penelope since Emmett had come over a few days earlier. Gabe had been busier than normal at work, not to mention something was bugging him. The past few months he had been acting strange, but whenever they asked what was going on, he never told them the truth. He always said everything was fine. Yet, he and Emmett both knew that was a lie.

He figured Emmett must've bugged Gabe, so here he was.

"Got something on your mind, Gabe?"

Gabe relaxed into the couch. "No. You?"

"Subtle, dude," Dare said with a chuckle. "He's fine. We were thinking about getting a drink. Do you want to tag along?"

That was the second time Dare popped in to take control of the situation. Did he need Dare stepping in when it was his brother Gabe? Shy, quiet, always friendly Gabe, who didn't like confrontation whatsoever.

The tension relaxed in Gabe's posture.

Maybe it *was* better Dare stepped in.

"Yeah, I could use a beer, I guess." He sighed heavily.

Yeah, he wished his brother would tell him what was going on with him. He didn't like seeing him so stressed out. And about what?

Of course, he didn't want to talk about Penelope, so what right did he have to keep pestering Gabe about sharing his problems?

He stood up, deciding he would leave Gabe alone about whatever was bothering him. "Let's hit the road. I bet we'll find some beautiful women tonight. It's always hopping on a Thursday at Chico's."

Dare stood up, yet the low groan didn't go unnoticed. He didn't want to pick up any women tonight. He didn't feel worthy enough.

Ethan also didn't miss the wince that fluttered across his brother Gabe's face. Apparently, his brother didn't want to meet any women either. No real surprise there. He was shy when it came to dating.

Meeting and chatting it up with other women had no real appeal for him either. But he said they were going, so he had to follow through.

It didn't take long to get to the bar, and the moment they stepped inside, his eyes zeroed in on Penelope.

Well, damn.

Not exactly what he wanted to deal with tonight.

"I see an open table near the pool tables. I'll grab—" Dare stopped speaking when he noticed the agony and the anger plastered on his face. "Ethan?"

He might not want to deal with it, but seeing her sitting at a table with Deja, Sophie, and Ava, all three of them laughing up a storm, it hit him.

They were laughing at *him*.

She was making him look like a fool. Talking about him. Saying what a mistake he was.

Without thinking about the consequences, he headed straight for her table.

5

PENELOPE'S HAND tightened on the glass filled to the rim with a strawberry daiquiri when the last man she wanted to see stopped right next to her. The anger etched on his face didn't bode well for her.

She wasn't ready to deal with him quite yet.

After the bomb she dropped, taking one round of shots with Deja and Ava since Sophie didn't drink alcohol, she told them what happened. How sorry she had been when she jumped to the wrong conclusions and the terrible words she said.

All three had encouraged her to speak to him and apologize, that he'd understand.

But looking at the fury etched across his handsome face she didn't think he would even stop for a second to listen to her.

"What a surprise seeing you here, Ethan," Deja said with a friendly tone, yet with a hint of caution. She quickly looked around the bar, then met his gaze again. "You're here with Dare and Gabe. Are they coming to say hi to us, too?"

Ethan didn't look away from Penelope as Deja spoke. "What are you doing?"

Her heart started to lightly pound. Her hand holding the glass trembled. "I don't know what you mean."

"You do know what I mean. What the hell have you been saying to them?"

Sophie cleared her throat. "Language please, Ethan."

Penelope heard a slight quiver in Sophie's tone of voice, and she glanced at her new friend, confused.

But it also distracted Ethan, who finally had the grace to look ashamed by his behavior.

"I'm sorry, Soph." He smiled. Not a true wonderful smile that Penelope loved, but a tiny one to appease Sophie.

"It's okay. I can see you're upset. I've never seen you upset like this, but this conversation could wait for another time," Sophie said calmly, yet still with a slight quiver in her tone.

"What Sophie is saying in a nice way," Ava piped in, her face filled with irritation, "is to knock it the hell off."

Sophie coughed.

Ava waved a hand at her. "Oh, sometimes nasty swear words need to be used, Sophie, and I didn't even use a nasty one." Then she leveled a stern gaze at Ethan. "Cool it. You can speak to Penelope about what happened between you two another time."

"So you know everything?"

Penelope closed her eyes at the pain in his voice.

"I don't know—"

"Yes, I shared everything with them," Penelope said, cutting off Ava as she snapped her gaze to his.

He met her eyes with a solemn expression mingled with hatred.

Oh, he truly hated her now.

Suddenly, his facial features morphed into indifference. "I loved you, Penelope. I've always loved you. But back then, it wasn't enough. And I'm starting to see that no matter what I do or what I say, it still won't be enough."

"Ethan—" She stopped speaking when the right words wouldn't surface. The last thing she wanted to do was say the wrong thing again.

He closed his eyes for a brief second as a long sigh escaped. "Forget it. It's clearly not going to work between us." Then he glanced around the table. "Enjoy the rest of your night continuing to laugh at me."

Then he walked away.

Her mouth dropped open as she watched him walk away. He stopped to say a few things to Dare and his brother Gabe and then walked out of the bar alone.

"Wow. That was...interesting," Deja said. "Why in the world would he think we were laughing at him? We would never do that."

"Because it's not the first time people have laughed at his expense."

Penelope jumped, startled, surprised to see Gabe standing next to her as he answered Deja's question in a soft tone.

"Nice to see you, Penelope."

Was it? Because Gabe didn't sound happy to see her.

"You, too, Gabe."

"Care to explain what you mean, Gabe?" Ava asked.

She waited, as did everyone else, even Dare who took a spot to stand between Deja and Sophie for Gabe to answer.

"No."

Gabe left it at that. He always had been a guy of few words. People always chalked it up to being shy, but Pene-lope thought it was more in terms of he liked to choose his words carefully. And if he didn't have anything to say, then he didn't speak.

But what did she know?

"We won't bother you anymore. Enjoy your evening." Then Gabe walked away, obviously assuming Dare would follow.

"Where did Ethan go?" Ava asked before Dare could walk away.

"It doesn't matter. He left. We only came out..." He cleared his throat, refusing to look at her. "We only came out for Ethan. But I don't want to talk about it. And Gabe's in a mood. Like he usually is."

"Yeah, something's been bothering him lately, but no matter who bugs him about it, he won't 'fess up. Says there's nothing to worry about," Ava replied.

Deja averted everyone's gaze, although Penelope figured she meant to do it unobtrusively, she caught it right away. Interesting. If Penelope had to guess, Deja knew exactly what was bothering Gabe.

Not her problem.

Because she wasn't a part of this family, no matter how much she wanted to be.

Before she screwed everything up earlier, she probably could've been. Because Ethan still loved her.

But not anymore.

"Well, you ladies enjoy. We won't bother you again." Dare grinned and walked away.

"Are you okay, Penelope?" Sophie asked quietly, her tone of voice indicating she cared. These three barely knew her. Why would they care about her?

She nodded but stood up, her drink not even close to being finished. "I'm going to call a cab and head home. It's been a very long day, and I'm tired. I don't want to ruin the rest of your evening."

"Once Ethan has time to cool down, I'm sure you two can talk things out. I don't know the entire history between you two, but it's easy to see you both care about each other. He even admitted he still loves you." Ava put a comforting hand on her arm.

"Yeah, talking has never been his forte. I don't think we'll be working anything out. I do appreciate you ladies listening to me, though. This was nice."

"And we'll do it again soon," Deja insisted.

Penelope tried to smile, even a tiny little grin. Nothing would come. "No, Deja. This won't happen again. It's better if I don't come around you. I hope you understand."

Perhaps she rendered them speechless because nobody said a word. Or maybe they simply agreed.

She grabbed her purse and left the bar, waiting outside in the chilly night for her cab to arrive.

The past month had been a month from hell.

Her dad died.

Ethan stormed back into her life and right back out.

And she survived—

No. She couldn't think about it because then she might have an attack and she couldn't lose control until she was inside and locked up tight in her house.

Yes, locked up tight.

She was never leaving her house again.

It was safer.

Safer for her well-being.

Safer for her livelihood.

Definitely safer for her heart.

Swinging his arm high, afraid he'd lose the last shred of energy he had left if he didn't do it quickly, he hung his helmet back up.

Coming into work early had helped focus his mind on something else, but it also left him tired as hell. The tension and fighting between Penelope and he left him raw and exhausted. Fighting another fire that looked to be the start of the work of an arsonist didn't help.

This was the third building set on fire in the past two weeks.

The first one had been an old house sitting on the outskirts of town, long ago abandoned. At first glance, it didn't look like anything suspicious occurred. It was an old house surrounded by dry fields. But then they saw signs that an accelerant was used to start the fire. After the arson investigator completed a thorough investigation, they determined gasoline was spread throughout the house. The flames ignited without pause. They didn't save much of the house from ruin. By the time they got there, it was engulfed in flames.

The second fire occurred closer to town, an old shed behind a gas station. Again, gasoline was used to start the fire, and not much of the shed remained standing. Thankfully, they got there in time before the fire spread to the gas station and the pumps. That could've been a huge disaster in the making.

The latest fire had hit the restroom area at the local playground. Thankfully, it had been later in the evening, which meant nobody had gotten hurt.

It had taken them quite a while to put out the latest fire. Since the last two fires, everyone had been on high alert. Whoever was starting these fires wasn't going to stop, and they were getting more brazen.

One of these times they might actually start a fire to a building with people in it.

So far, they had no witnesses, and no leads to the perp.

Taking off the rest of his gear, he hung it up and walked to the break room for a nice cold drink. Between working with heavy equipment, being in close proximity to the flaming beast, and exerting all his strength, he was always thirsty afterward. He usually drank at least three large glasses of water before he felt more hydrated and centered.

He also liked to take a shower, and he could at the station, but at the moment he didn't have the energy for much. His mind was so drained. He wanted to lie down for a week and never get out of bed until all the bad in his life disappeared.

Ethan drank his first two glasses of ice-cold water, a nice full pitcher waiting in the fridge for him, and filled his glass up one more time.

"Crazy, huh? People are psychos," Gene said, a fellow coworker who'd been out there battling the fire, as he joined him in the break room.

In the last few weeks, it seemed they had been busier than usual. Of course, with the arsonist running around, Ethan didn't foresee his workload getting any easier or quieter any time soon—not until they caught the perp.

"Yep, they are." Ethan drained his last glass of water, feeling marginally better.

"You okay? You looked distracted when you came in. And you came in early."

Ethan set his glass in the sink. "Right as rain. I'm itching to catch this bastard."

"Oh, we all are, buddy. But you usually don't come in early. What's up? Don't ignore me."

But he was so good at ignoring his feelings. He wanted to

ignore everything until it all went away. He needed to occupy his mind again. Not that he wanted another fire to pop up, but he could clean equipment or organize downstairs. Anything to get his mind off Penelope.

"I'm good, man. I just wanted to come in early."

Gene clapped him on the back. "Somehow I doubt that, but I'm not going to keep bugging you."

Ethan nodded, thankful his friend understood. Gene walked out of the break room, leaving him all by himself. The silence surrounded him, filling him with despair so brutal and gut-wrenching, he felt like getting sick.

He headed downstairs to get some things done around the station, but the noise from some of the other guys downstairs hit him the wrong way just like the silence upstairs did. He felt stuck in a weird limbo where everything felt off-kilter.

Turning around, he decided to take a shower and wash off the ugliness from the day—from the fighting with Penelope to the fire that destroyed a part of his town. He took his time letting the water rain down over him, yet he didn't feel an ounce of cleanliness when he was all finished. He still felt dirty and distraught.

Instead of joining his coworkers, he lay down on his bunk and let his mind wander to Penelope.

Sweet, assertive Penelope.

Yet, something wasn't quite right with her.

He saw her hand tremble at the bar tonight when he got in her face. As if she had been on the verge of another panic attack like she had earlier in the day in her car.

Because of him?

He hated to think so.

As much as he wanted to hate her with a passion, he didn't. He couldn't.

She would always have a hold on his heart, even if he despised the very idea.

She had ruined him from loving another woman. Although, in all honesty, he hadn't tried very hard to love another woman. Because every time he looked at any woman, gorgeous in their own right, he always compared them to Penelope.

From the moment he bumped into her coming out of the locker room in high school, he had been stunned by her beauty. She didn't just knock into him. She knocked a whole bout of love in his heart that wouldn't disappear. Always, no matter what he did to try and forget her, the love punctured his heart.

Which made everything hurt worse.

She laughed at him.

They all did.

Starting right this second, he'd wipe her from his mind. Thinking about her wouldn't solve anything. It wouldn't change anything.

He loved Penelope Justice.

He just couldn't have her.

6

"GIMME ALL THE DAMN MONEY. *Let's go!*"

Penelope pressed her face closer to the floor, practically kissing it as the man shouted at the teller behind the counter.

"Dude, hurry it up. I hear sirens," another man said from behind her, closer to the exit.

Of all the days she had to stop at the bank for cash, it had to be today. She should've just paid the ATM fee and grabbed the money she needed right next to her office building. Because then she wouldn't be lying face down on the ground in the middle of a bank robbery.

"Hurry it up, bitch. Did you hear my brother?"

She squeezed her eyes shut tighter when the teller screamed. Part of her wanted to lift her head and find out why she screamed. But the smart part of her kept her eyes closed and her head down.

The second the men burst into the building brandishing their weapons, hollering for everyone to get down on the floor, she complied. She wasn't an idiot. They went person to person, about five to ten people in the lobby, grabbing their phones and shoving them all into a nylon bag. Then one went to the young teller

behind the counter—she had to only be in her early twenties—
and demanded she empty her cash register. The other stood near
the exit keeping an eye out.

She'd seen so many cases in law school where it didn't end
well for the victims, and she knew better than to try anything
stupid. It's why she chose corporate law instead of criminal law.
She didn't have the ferocity to deal with criminals.

Suddenly, a sharp ache tore through her head when a rough
hand grabbed a handful of hair and yanked her to her feet. She let
out a cry of terror.

"You have five seconds to finish up with all the money, or I
blow this chick's brains out. Do you hear me?" the man yelled as
he pressed a gun to the side of her head.

The cold metal from the gun sent a shiver down her spine so
strong and fierce, she was afraid she may pass out.

The man jerked her hard against his frame. "Don't move,
bitch. The gun might go off."

Biting her lip hard enough that she tasted blood, she tried to
hold herself as steady as possible. She knew the man meant business. He wasn't joking around.

"Five. Four. Three. Two..." The pressure from the gun intensi-
fied, and a tiny squeak left her mouth. "Do you hear that, lady?
This woman doesn't want to die. Are you finished?"

Although she was standing up, free to see everything going
around her, she had yet to open her eyes. She was too terrified to
look.

In that chaotic moment, her mind conjured one thing—the
only thing she wanted to see before she died.

Ethan McCord.

No matter how much time passed, he was always in her
thoughts, in her heart. She had so many regrets. One of them
being—

"Shit, man. She dropped a bunch on the floor," the brother said, standing near the counter.

The man cocked the gun. The deadly sound and the cold metal pressed against her clammy skin sent a shockwave through her system.

"One."

A shot fired.

———

PENELOPE BOLTED UPRIGHT IN BED, sweat dripping from her pores. The covers were tangled around her legs, and her pillow wasn't behind her head where it belonged. Rolling slightly, shoving the covers off, she leaned over the side of the bed and grabbed her pillow from the floor.

It wasn't the first time she'd had the nightmare in the past month since the terrible ordeal happened. Every time, her pillow always ended up on the floor. Because she fought in her sleep, as she had fought in real life.

She won the fight. The bad guys lost.

Yet, every new day felt like she came out the loser.

Punching her pillow a few times, she closed her eyes and tried to fall back asleep. After several minutes of tossing and turning, punching her pillow to find a comfortable position, she knew it was useless.

She was never going to fall back asleep.

She never could after one of her nightmares, reliving a horror she hated thinking about.

Climbing out of bed, she changed into a T-shirt and sweatpants and grabbed a pair of socks from the dresser drawer.

The stars still twinkled in the sky, but she had to get out of the house. She needed to relieve some of her pent-up emotions. She hadn't left the house in the past four days—not since the awkward outburst in the bar with Ethan. She hadn't even ventured out to check her mail; that's how much she'd locked herself inside like a recluse.

Deja knocked on the door yesterday. She only knew it was her because she had walked up to the door, in the most stealth-like manner she could, and looked through the peephole to confirm who it was. Even though she felt bad ignoring her knocks, she didn't answer the door.

She didn't want Deja to ask how she was doing, how she was feeling, do you want to go out again? She didn't want to answer any questions about whether she had seen Ethan yet. She didn't want to deal with anything.

Tying her shoes tight, she grabbed a water bottle from the fridge and took a long swallow before returning it. Glancing at the microwave clock, she hesitated—3:33 a.m.

Was it safe to be running outside this early in the morning?

Probably not.

Oh, well. She survived a bank robbery with a gun pointed at her head; running early in the morning in the dark couldn't be much worse.

Since the numbers hadn't changed yet, she made a wish like she always had when she was a little girl. Any time the clock hit the same numbers, she made a wish. It was something fun she and her mom had done. Penelope's mom passed away in a freak car accident, and though she always wished her mom could come back, it never happened. People couldn't come back from the dead, no matter how desperately she wished they could. If it were possible, she'd wish both of her parents back to her.

Pushing her silly wish aside, she grabbed her phone and her house key and set off running.

The cool morning air sent a chill through her spine, yet it also urged her on. Soon, after a few minutes of running, she was at a nice steady pace, and the coldness barely affected her.

Emptying her mind of everything—her nightmare, Ethan McCord, the mess her life was in, every single thing that plagued her with worries—she ran.

She ran like someone was chasing her.

When it finally felt like her chest was about to explode, she slowed her pace until she came to a complete stop. Resting her hands on her knees, gulping in large breaths of air, she wondered how she was going to make it back home.

Crazy laughter filtered the air as she stood and glanced around. She didn't recognize the neighborhood. Quite a few neighborhoods had popped up since she left town nine years ago. Of course, that's what happened all over the country. New developments here and there until there was no more room left for anything else.

The area looked like it was still in the building phase. A new community that would bring in more people, most likely families.

She had no family left.

Sure, she had an aunt and uncle living up north and another aunt living in Chicago, but she rarely saw them. And the sprinkle of cousins she had, she probably wouldn't even recognize them if they crossed her path. The only people she had been close with was her mom and dad, and then just her dad when her mom passed away when she was eight.

Would she ever have a family of her own?

She didn't think so. Because the only man she wanted to build a life with hated her.

Rotating her shoulders, preparing to head home,

praying she wouldn't collapse before that happened, she paused when she saw a weird flicker.

Strange.

She swore she saw a light, maybe a flashlight coming from one of the partially built homes.

Instead of moving in the direction of her house, she found herself moving toward the light that had mysteriously disappeared.

Another stupid move by her. Most definitely. If she were truly smart, she would call the police.

But what if it was her eyes playing tricks on her? She should be sure before she called the cops and it turned out to be nothing.

As soon as she crossed the street and stood in front of the house, she knew there was no avoiding calling 9-1-1.

Her eyes were not playing tricks on her.

And it wasn't a flashlight either.

The house was on fire.

She grabbed her phone from her pocket as her heart started to lightly pound and dialed three numbers she hated even thinking about.

"9-1-1, what's your emergency?"

An odd sound from her right had her twisting her head.

But she was too late to react.

A black figure stood in front of her and whacked her on the side of the head.

The last thing she heard before crumpling to the ground was the same words repeated again. "9-1-1, what's your emergency?"

THROWING AN ARM OVER HIS EYES, Ethan suppressed a groan before moving his arm back to his side. No matter how many times he turned this way or shifted that way, he still couldn't get to sleep.

He supposed it didn't help he was at the fire station lying on one of the cots instead of his own bed. It was his own fault, too. He asked for the extra shift.

Because being at home, around his family, was not what he wanted. And he refused to drown himself in alcohol so he decided he'd drown himself in work.

Of course, he wouldn't say he didn't love his family, because he did. He wouldn't say he didn't appreciate their concern, because he did.

But they needed to back off and mind their own damn business.

Four days had gone by since he last saw Penelope. Since he last acted like a jackass in front of her—and the last three people he should've. Ava hadn't stopped pestering him about his behavior, and Deja was no better. Sophie was the only one who hadn't bothered him, and he couldn't have been happier. Although, he didn't expect her to either. She didn't get into other people's business.

But her look of disapproval before he walked away from the table said enough. He'd disappointed her.

After plenty of time to ruminate and assess his actions, he didn't disagree with anyone's assessment.

He acted like a grade-A jackass.

He let his emotions get the better of him.

He let old wounds sink into his conscience and made him think they were laughing at him. Because when Penelope originally left, a few people laughed at him. Some of his friends. Some of her friends.

How come you let such a hottie leave you?

Why didn't you go with, idiot?

You screwed the pooch on that one, McCord.

She's better off without you, loser.

I always told her it wouldn't last.

Each time they laughed like jackals after delivering their so-called advice and cruel words.

What the hell was he supposed to think after the things Penelope said to him after the most amazing sex they had? Then to see her laughing with three women he was surprised to see her sitting with. It made sense when he first saw everything.

He knew he should apologize for his behavior—again. He just didn't know how to get the words out, or how to approach her.

Her words were loud and clear.

They might've had sex, but he was a mistake. So why bother apologizing.

The more he tried to get her out of his mind, the more she slipped in and took control of his entire being. He couldn't get rid of any of his distracting thoughts. Sweet, sexy images of her underneath him, moaning with delight. Her gorgeous smile, smirking at him like she knew what he was thinking. Most of the time, she did. He didn't think nine years changed that.

Around and around his thoughts went.

Even at damn near four o'clock in the morning. Good thing his shift ended in two hours. He could go home and toss and turn in his own bed. Comfortable or not, he knew he wouldn't get a wink of sleep.

Just as he started to shift to his side, a loud siren pierced the quiet.

Jumping out of bed, fully clothed and ready to go, he ran for his gear.

Definitely not how he wanted to spend the end of his shift, but at least his mind would stop conjuring thoughts of Penelope.

It didn't take long to don on his turnout gear and snag his position on the firetruck alongside his coworkers. No matter the crew he worked with, they were a well-oiled machine, working together like they'd been doing it since birth.

A few minutes later, considering the call wasn't too far from the fire station, they came upon a new community in the cusp of development. One of the semi-built homes was on fire. As soon as the scene unveiled in front of him, he knew it was the work of their serial arsonist. They had yet to catch or find a viable piece of evidence to find the perp. By the expressions on his coworkers' faces as they worked to get the hose out and tame the roaring beast, they were thinking the same thing.

Surprisingly, they were able to dowse the flames rather quickly and save part of the house. It would still need to be rebuilt, but the fire didn't destroy it all.

They actually made it in time before it was fully engulfed in flames. How odd. They never reached the fire as fast as this before.

Throwing off his helmet after he noticed Officer Malley nod at him, he told Gene he'd be right back to help clean up.

"Hey, Ethan. You guys were quick."

"The call came in quick. Not too far from the station either. I guess this guy is getting pretty brazen."

Officer Malley shook his head as if he agreed whoever they were dealing with was getting a little too ballsy. Then he nodded toward his left where an ambulance sat. It was the first time Ethan even noticed it sitting there. When did it arrive?

"I thought you might want to know who called it in." Officer Malley winced. "Penelope Justice."

Ethan had been looking at Officer Malley, but as soon as he said Penelope's name, his attention jerked toward the ambulance. He didn't even wait to ask him any questions. His feet started moving and didn't stop until he stood inches from her sitting perched on the back of the ambulance with white gauze pressed firmly to the side of her head.

"Penelope, are you okay? What are you doing here? What happened?" The questions filtered out in rapid fire. By the fear and panic in her eyes, he knew he shouldn't have approached her in such a manner, but he couldn't help it.

He needed answers. He needed to know she was okay. If he ever lost her—

Shit, she wasn't his, to begin with. But if something happened to her—well, he didn't want to think about it.

When she didn't respond but continued to look at him with her eyes glazed over in terror, he brushed a hand across her cheek before dropping it back to his side.

"I'm sorry. I didn't mean to pelt you with questions. How can I help?"

A harsh shiver rippled throughout her entire body. "Take me home...please." Her plea came out in a terrified whisper.

He nodded, touching her knee casually before turning around to find Officer Malley and get some answers. Except he wasn't too far away from him, smiling with a goofy smirk as if he knew he wouldn't be too long.

He touched her knee again, this time squeezing lightly in reassurance. He wanted to touch her cheek or enfold her in a hug or kiss her sweet lips, but he knew it wasn't his place. But he had to touch her. He had to show his support, that she wasn't alone in whatever happened. Because the horrified look in her eyes said she was floating in a pool of misery all alone. He wasn't leaving her until he knew why she looked so lost and afraid.

"I'll be right back, and then I'll take you home. I promise."

He stepped away and stopped in front of Officer Malley. "What the hell happened?"

"Well, I was going to tell you, and you walked away too soon. She was running, going for a late-night run, or more like, early-morning jog, and she stopped here to turn around. She saw a light coming from the house and went to investigate. When she got closer, she noticed the house was on fire and dialed 9-1-1. Before she could respond to the operator, some guy came out of nowhere and knocked her out." Officer Malley sighed. "She's lucky he didn't hurt her any more than he did. She's extremely lucky. Maybe tell her it's not the best idea to run so late at night."

Ethan's heart started to pound at the implications, at the nasty scenarios that could've happened instead of just a hit to the head. The arsonist could've tossed her inside the burning building. Oh, yeah. He'd be having a lengthy chat with her about running so late at night all alone.

"Did she get a good look at the guy?"

Officer Malley shook his head. "Only that he was wearing all black. It happened too fast, she said."

"I'm taking her home." Ethan glanced around and saw the paramedic talking to Penelope. "Unless she needs to go to the hospital, then I'm escorting her there."

"I think it was just a nasty bump. You'll have to talk to Gus about whether she needs to go to the hospital."

Ethan patted his shoulder and grinned, even though he

didn't want to pretend like everything was okay. Because nothing was okay. Everything was all wrong, especially the fact Penelope was sitting in the back of an ambulance with an injury. "I appreciate everything. I'm glad you got here as fast as you did."

Ethan spoke to Gus, the paramedic, and reassured him that he'd stay with Penelope to monitor any signs for a concussion. Thankfully, she only suffered a minor scrape and her wound didn't require stitches. Otherwise, she'd have to take a trip to the hospital. By the panicked look in her eyes every time Gus mentioned the hospital, Ethan knew that wasn't the best option. So he made it known quite clearly he wouldn't leave her side for anything.

He spoke to his captain about everything going on and got permission to leave the site. He didn't get any flack or disapproving glares from any of his coworkers for leaving.

Bundling Penelope in a blanket borrowed from the ambulance, he asked Officer Malley for a ride to her house.

Before long, he had Penelope home, changed into new clothes, and tucked into bed. He needed to change, though, considering he still had on his fire gear.

But she wasn't having that. When he tried to stand up from her bed, she grabbed his hand.

"Don't leave me. Please, Ethan. Don't leave me."

Sitting back down on the soft bed, a bed he couldn't dismiss from his mind, he squeezed her hand.

"Never, Penelope. I'm staying right here."

And if he had his way, he'd never leave her again.

Whatever issues they had, they could work through. He knew it.

Because he loved Penelope Justice.

Always and forever.

7

Penelope woke up slowly, the smell of bacon drifting her way. Glancing at the clock on the nightstand, she saw it was nearing one o'clock in the afternoon. She didn't know how long she'd been out, considering Ethan wouldn't let her sleep more than two hours at a time, but it was enough to feel slightly better.

Her head still ached where the man hit her, but it wasn't as bad as it was when it originally happened.

Taking her time to sit up, a wave of dizziness hit her. Closing her eyes, placing a hand on her forehead, she waited a few seconds before opening her eyes again. The room didn't spin, but she felt off-kilter.

Well, what did she do now? Calling out for Ethan sounded pathetic. Sitting in bed waiting for him to check on her sounded pathetic. Standing up and falling on her ass from dizziness sounded pathetic.

Overall, she was pathetic. And an idiot.

She should've called the police right away. Instead, she got hurt by some stranger, and it could've been so much worse.

She closed her eyes again.

How would she face Ethan after this? How would she face herself in the mirror was the better question. Why did she keep putting herself in dangerous situations? Although, in her defense, she had no control over the bank robbery. That was bad luck. Wrong place, wrong time.

She heard the footsteps before she felt the bed dip down, and yet, she couldn't open her eyes. She couldn't see the look of disgust in Ethan's eyes.

Then a warm hand caressed her cheek and didn't disappear until her eyes finally popped open.

"Are you okay? You look a little pale." Ethan rubbed her cheek softly one more time before letting his hand drift down to his side.

"I sat up and got a little dizzy. Nothing serious." She averted her gaze. "Thank you for everything. I appreciate it."

"Of course. I'll always help you."

Her eyes shot to his. "Seriously? You hate me."

Ethan stood up from the bed, which did nothing but reinforce her words that he hated her. But then his hand reached out toward her.

"Come on. Something to eat might help. I made you breakfast."

She stared at his hand for the longest time before looking up into his soulful, concerned eyes. Then she grabbed his hand and let him help her up. The dizziness attacked her again, but not as bad as the first time and not as bad with Ethan's help.

He curled an arm around her waist and helped her out of her room. With each step she took, she felt better. She honestly didn't think she needed his help the entire way there, but she liked his hands on her. She wanted to savor the moment, even if it wouldn't last.

He finally let go when they reached the table, and she sat down. Such a gentleman, he even scooted the chair in for her.

A feast fit for a queen sat in front of her. Eggs, toast, bacon, hash browns, three slices of French toast, and a nice cold glass of orange juice. The moment the wonderful aroma of bacon woke her up, she knew she would devour every bite.

Ethan pulled out a chair next to her and sat down, his own plate in front of him.

"This is a lot of food." She didn't mean it in an offensive way, but unfortunately, it might've come out in a brusque tone by the way he cocked a brow.

"I wasn't sure what you might want. You don't have to eat it all."

She nodded, unsure of what to say. Her tone could have been friendlier. But she wasn't sure why he was acting all nice and cooperative when the last time she saw him, he acted like he hated her.

For the first time, she noticed he didn't have on his fire gear. Of course, he wouldn't. That would've been uncomfortable to wear all day. But when did he leave? She remembered quite vividly begging him not to leave her alone. It didn't get much more pathetic than that.

"You changed," she said quietly as she scooped a bite of eggs onto her fork.

"My buddy swung by with a change of clothes and grabbed my gear for me. I also took a shower." Ethan went silent after that, eating his food, glancing her way every few seconds.

She didn't know what else to say, so she stayed silent and ate her food. Delicious food, too; Ethan was a good cook. There was so much food on her plate, she didn't think she'd eat it all. Except, no more than ten minutes later, her entire plate was cleared except for a few bites of toast and one remaining slice of French toast.

Ethan's fork clanged against his plate at the same time hers did. Their eyes met.

"I don't hate you." He released a heavy sigh as he rubbed the few days' growth on his chin. "I'm sorry about the way I acted at the bar. I was out of line and...I apologize."

She swallowed—the words clogged in her throat. What did she say to that? She never imagined he'd apologize to her.

"I'm sorry, too. I never should've ruined..." Well, she wanted to say a beautiful moment, but she couldn't. What would he say to that? "I didn't mean what I said after..."

She was mucking up her apology so badly.

His hand tentatively reached out across the table. "Penelope...can we be friends?"

Friends?

He just wanted to be friends?

Her heart started to pound fiercely as the anger welled up inside.

Well, she didn't like it because she loved the big dummy, but she'd take it. Being friends was better than being enemies, and he was obviously accepting her apology.

Her hand met his, their fingers interlocking. "Friends."

A bright, brilliant smile lit up his gorgeous face. Oh, boy, did she love his handsome, sexy smile.

Then his smile disappeared in a blink of an eye, replaced with an angry scowl. His hand tightened around hers.

"If you are ever that stupid again, I'm going to spank your ass hard."

Her mouth dropped open at his forceful, demanding

words. Who the hell did he think he was speaking to her like that?

Before she could slash him with her brutal tongue, his hand squeezed hers again. She knew right away; it was to comfort her because she was shaking like a leaf. Because he was right. It *was* stupid of her to go running so early in the morning.

"I wanted to clear my head. I know it was dumb to go running so late at night." A picture of his hands caressing her ass before smacking it hard flashed before her eyes. Her body responded in kind, her insides melting with pleasure. "And I'll take the punishment freely." She smiled wickedly. "As friends, of course."

His angry scowl vanished as delicious intent lit up his eyes. "I thought you'd berate me for hollering at you. I'm glad you see it my way."

She stood and grabbed her plate. "Well, don't think I'll always see it your way. But in this instance, you were right. It was dumb of me."

She walked away before more blurted out of her mouth. Like how much worse it could've been. She got lucky a month ago. She got lucky this morning. How much luck did she have left?

Ethan followed closely behind her, setting his nearly empty plate right next to hers on the counter.

"Are you okay? How is the dizziness?"

She grabbed the counter, not because a bout of dizziness was attacking her, but because of the concern in his tone.

But why wouldn't he be concerned? They were friends now. He apologized. He didn't hate her.

Yet, she wanted it to be so much more than that.

"I'm feeling better. You were right. The food helped." Then she let go of the counter and turned toward him with a cheery smile when she felt nothing close to happiness. "You don't have to stay with me anymore. I'll be okay. I promise."

"When twenty-four hours rolls around, then I'll go. Until then," he said with a sexy-as-sin grin as he leaned against the counter, "you're stuck with me."

Well, she could handle that, of course. Not that she'd let him know how much she'd enjoy for him to stay.

"I mean, if you want. It's not a big deal." Then she shrugged for added measure, so he completely understood she didn't care either way. She didn't.

Ethan's expression softened, and not in a sexual, let-me-love-your-body kind of way. "Officer Malley said you didn't get a good look at the guy. Anything jogging your memory now?"

Like a bolt of lightning striking her dead center, her mind flashed vivid memories.

But not of the attack this morning.

From the memories she tried so hard to forget.

Everything went black.

ETHAN BARELY CAUGHT Penelope before she crashed to the floor. One moment he was asking her a question—one he didn't think was too traumatic—and the next, she fainted on him.

Cradling her sweet, delectable body close to his, he carried her back to her bedroom and laid her down gently.

He sat there watching her, waiting for her to wake back up, wondering if he should take her to the hospital. First, dizziness. Now, this.

When he was about to pick her up and rush her out of

the house, her eyes started to blink, and then her gaze met his.

"I should take you to the hospital, Penelope." Because he couldn't control himself, his hand found her cheek and softly caressed it.

He found it difficult to keep his hands to himself earlier. Sure, he touched her cheek lightly, helped her walk to the dining room table, held her hand, but he never wanted to let go any of those times. He only wanted to hold her and pretend nothing disastrous ever occurred between them.

But he couldn't do that. He couldn't do anything he wanted with her because they were just friends.

Just. Friends.

Damn. He was the stupidest man alive to even utter those words. He didn't even know why he did. The only thought that went through his mind as she looked ready to kick him out when he apologized for his behavior was he didn't want to lose her in any way. So if being friends was the only way he could keep her in his life, then that's what he'd do.

"Penelope?" He repeated her name when she didn't respond.

"Sorry, what did you say?" She bit her bottom lip, the simple act entirely too enticing. "It's hard to think when..."

His thumb wouldn't stop brushing her cheek, which had slowly begun turning a bright shade of red. "When what?"

"When my friend touches me like this."

That had him removing his hand in a flash.

He couldn't quite decipher her words. Whether they were meant in a teasing tone or she was berating him for touching her in more than a friendly manner.

"You fainted. I think we should go to the hospital." It

would be better if he focused on the problem at hand and not at how much he wanted to kiss her sweet, red lips that looked like they were ready for him to devour.

She averted his gaze. "I'm fine. It was nothing."

"Penelope." He said her name rather sharply so she would look at him. "You fainted. That's not nothing. This man, whoever attacked you, is dangerous. He could've hurt you so much worse. Did you see his face? Is that why you fainted?"

Her head tentatively moved back and forth.

Okay. Odd. Because he believed her. But the fear in her eyes said something terrifying made her faint.

"Talk to me. I can help."

"You can't."

His hand started to reach for her again, but he stopped himself before he made contact. "I can. I can do anything I put my mind to."

"Can you?"

His brows drew low, puzzled by the question. But her tone of voice said plenty. "Meaning?"

She suddenly smiled and reached out to him this time, patting his knee. "I'm fine. It was a silly fainting spell, but nothing serious. I'd like to take a shower. Why don't you do the dishes?"

Interesting. She was trying to avoid him. Avoid the problem, more like it.

He didn't want to let her out of his sight, not after she just fainted, but he also knew he had no say in the matter. If she wanted to walk away from him, he wouldn't be able to stop her.

Fine, then.

As soon as she got out of the shower, he'd interrogate

her. He had less than twenty-four hours to find out what was on her mind.

He didn't think it had anything to do with this recent attack.

8

DRESSING in the shabbiest pair of sweatpants she owned and the rattiest T-shirt she could find, she walked out of her bedroom and found Ethan in the living room lounging on the couch with the sports channel on.

"Still a baseball fan, I see," she said with a chuckle as she took a seat on the couch, but made sure it was with plenty of space between them.

An adorable grin lit up his face. "I will always and forever be a baseball fan." His eyes grazed up and down her body before he said, "Feel better?"

"I do. It's amazing how much a shower can make you feel refreshed. And not one dizzy spell."

"Good. I'm glad to hear that, otherwise I would've had to forcibly remove you from the house and take you to the hospital."

"No spanking this time?" she asked with a teasing grin. She didn't even know why she asked because it was playing with fire.

They were friends.

Only friends.

But it was so hard to remember.

His grin inched up a notch. "Spanking is reserved for more erroneous behavior."

"Duly noted," she said with a sexy smile she couldn't contain.

He scooted over a bit, within arm's reach. "So, Penelope..."

She couldn't help herself. She moved over his way. "Yes, Ethan?"

"Why don't you tell me the real reason you fainted? And I don't think it's because of what happened this morning."

Her smile fell. Her happiness dissipated. Her mood took a nose dive. Because that was the one thing she didn't want to talk about. The entire shower she tried not only to clean off the terrible events from the morning but also the bad memories from a month ago.

He moved again, grabbing her hand this time. And for the life of her, she couldn't stop the trembles.

"You can tell me anything, Penelope. Even though we've had our...disagreements lately, you can talk to me. Something's bothering you." His hand tightened as it had before in a comforting way. "Something's been bothering you. That panic attack you almost had in the parking lot...I'm starting to think it wasn't about me."

She tried to jerk her hand away. "Ha! You would think everything is about you. Always about Ethan. Ethan, Ethan, Ethan."

She jerked again, but he refused to budge.

"Talk to me. I'm not that selfish, and you know it."

"Oh, really? We're going to have that talk, are we?"

His hand crushed hers as he leaned closer. "No, we're not deflecting this conversation. Tell me why you fainted. The real reason. I know when you're lying."

"So now you think you know me after nine years apart?"

"I'd know you down to your very core with fifty years apart. I love you, goddamnit!" he shouted, then his lips met hers.

Soul-crushing, piercing, and oh, so brutal. Yet, she felt the tenderness, the love, the aching gentleness as their tongues clashed and battled.

And as abruptly as he claimed her lips, he broke it off, backing away, breathing heavily.

"I love you, Penelope. I always have." His voice cracked. "I always will."

"But..." She didn't understand. He wanted friends only. He said so himself.

"But nothing. It's the truth." His eyes cast down to their locked hands. "And if you haven't noticed, I don't do communication well." Then his gaze zoomed to hers. "But it can't get much clearer than this. I love you. No matter what happens between us. I love you."

A lone tear slid down her cheek. It appeared before she could prevent it.

"Talk to me."

Maybe she should. Maybe she should finally talk to someone, even if he wasn't a professional. She didn't even confess to her dad what happened to her a month ago. When she thought about it, it was better all around. Because her dad died knowing his baby girl was okay when deep inside, she didn't feel close to being okay. She didn't know if she'd ever be okay.

"Penelope, please."

The ache in his tone. The plea in his voice. The despair in his eyes told her she should at least confess a little part of what happened.

Her mouth opened to speak.

Nothing came out.

"What happened?" Ethan asked softly. Like if he spoke any louder, she might not answer him at all.

This time she grabbed his hand, tightening the hold as if she were floating on a raft in the middle of the ocean, and if she let go for even a second, the water would swallow her up whole.

"Everything," she whispered desperately. "Everything happened."

ETHAN WAITED with bated breath for Penelope to keep speaking. He was afraid one wrong move or even one wrong word would have her backing away and hiding in the tight shell she had erected around herself.

Of course, his behavior and attitude toward her lately hadn't helped. But he would do anything, say anything to get her to open up and tell him what the hell was going on. Even if they would only be friends until the end of time, he wanted to help her in any way he could.

"About a month ago..."

Her words filtered out in a whisper.

He squeezed her hand in reassurance, yet said nothing.

"We were all supposed to donate money for a gift to our boss for her birthday. I don't carry cash on me. I use my debit card for everything, but I wasn't going to be the only person who didn't contribute to the gift."

She paused.

He waited patiently for her to continue. He felt like one wrong word, and she'd shut him out. This was good. He couldn't do anything to ruin the moment.

"I didn't want to stop at the ATM near my work because

it's not associated with my bank and I would've had to pay a stupid fee." She rolled her eyes. "Who wants to pay that fee?"

Instead of squeezing her hand like he had been doing, he raised it and kissed the back of it to let her know he understood. He understood everything. The need to save pennies where she could. The need to tell her story at her own pace. Every. Little. Thing.

"I stopped at my bank instead. Worse decision ever." Her voice hiccupped like she was trying to hold back tears. "I will always stop at an ATM these days. I don't care what the fee is."

She paused again.

Silence.

More silence.

The silence filled the room so much it made him sick to his stomach, yet he didn't say anything. He felt it bone-deep —if he said anything, she wouldn't finish her story.

"I was next in line. One more person to go and I would've been able to withdraw twenty dollars, because hey," she shrugged, "I liked my boss, I wanted to donate twenty dollars. Just one more person."

A terrible sinking feeling entered his gut. So strong and brutal, he wanted to get up and rush to the bathroom and get sick.

"They came out of nowhere. Two men with a gun." This time she didn't just hiccup, the tears flowed freely. "They demanded money from the teller, and they wanted our phones. I gave up mine willingly. I'm not dumb. Neither was anyone else. The teller was doing the best she could to get the money. But they kept yelling at her. Demanding she hurry up."

Penelope stopped speaking, the tears raining down her

face so strong he had a hard time deciphering what she was saying. But he understood quite clearly what happened. She had been a victim in a bank robbery.

He clasped his other hand over the top of hers but didn't say a word. He knew she understood he was comforting her and for her to continue at her own pace.

"One of the men grabbed me and put a gun to my head, hollering at the teller to go faster. It all happened so fast." Her dejected, soulful eyes met his. "The guy holding me was crazy. They told me afterward he was high, strung up on some heavy drugs. He fired a shot at the teller. It scared me, the loud bang. As soon as he fired, all hell broke loose. People started screaming, even me. But I also didn't hesitate to step on the inside of his foot and bring an elbow back into his gut. It was enough to loosen his hold and get out of his arms. I still had my purse in my hand, so I swung it around and connected with his head."

Her tears continued to mingle with her terrifying words. Ethan wanted to pelt question after question, yet he found the strength to remain silent. He knew she wasn't ready for that. By the evidence marring her face, she might not be ready anytime soon. The story was already taking a huge toll on her.

"I can't tell you everything. It's all such a blur. While I was fighting the man, the security guard pulled out a weapon hidden underneath his pant leg and shot the man near the teller window. Because I wasn't backing down from the guy I was fighting with, his gun fell out of his hand. I don't know what came over me, but I kept hitting him. Oh, and he didn't let me. He started fighting back. It was like that bar brawl we witnessed when we snuck into Haverty's bar that one time. You remember that?"

He nodded as he kissed her hand. He wanted to comfort

her, agree with her because he did remember, but he needed her to finish the story.

"I didn't get to beat the living shit out of him like I wanted because a few of the other customers in the bank stepped in and helped me. I survived. They survived. We all survived."

"Because you're one badass chick, Penelope." His words garnered a small smile in between her tears.

"The one brother died. The security guard had a good aim." She sighed heavily as she wiped her face with her free hand. "The other brother was arrested. I gave my statement and went on my way, even with the few bumps and bruises I received from the scuffle. But it..." More tears escaped. "It hit me harder than I realized. I quit my job, I moved home, and I hoped to carry on with my life with my dad helping me along the way. I needed to be with my dad..."

"Then, he died."

She nodded. "It was so sudden. Just like my mom."

Ethan couldn't stand it anymore. He scooted until he was able to smoothly grab her and place her on his lap, wrapping his arms around her securely. He wanted her to feel safe and secure. And not alone at all.

If he had his way, she'd never be alone again.

"No matter the issues between us, you are never alone. Ever. You have me. You'll always have me."

The tears were coming down so strong and fierce he had a hard time deciphering her words. But he managed to make it out. Because it was only two simple words.

"Do I?"

9

PENELOPE TIED HER SHOELACES, double-knotted, and then grabbed a bottle of water. Last time she ran, she ran so hard she felt like her heart was going to burst right out of her chest.

But this time she'd have water to help her gain her equilibrium back.

A month ago, she ran from her problems instead of meeting them head-on. She couldn't keep running from them.

Well, she was going running right now, but she wasn't running from her problems, she was facing them. So someone caught her unaware and knocked her out. It happened. She wasn't going to let it stop her from living, from doing what she wanted to do. And, right now, she wanted to go for a run.

Because she learned her lesson, she was going running with the bright sunlight shining down. Lunch passed, she had a simple salad with a banana and a glass of wine. Because, yeah, she wanted a glass.

As soon as she finished her jog, she was going to get

online and find a job. No more hiding. No more sulking. No more letting her fear and anxiety rule—because she refused to believe it was panic attacks assailing her—but she would live her life the way she wanted.

Of course, her change of heart might have something to do with Ethan, not that she'd ever admit it to the man.

Locking her front door, she didn't look back once as she started at a steady pace down the sidewalk.

Ethan was a lifesaver. She wasn't even sure he knew how much of a lifesaver he was.

One week ago, he brought her home, took care of her, and made her confess her deepest, darkest secret. Then she questioned his loyalty to her when he said he'd always be there for her. Since that moment, he hadn't backed down. He didn't disappear. He didn't make her wonder and worry at night that it was just words.

He spent the night, all platonic, of course, because she had a potential concussion. He made breakfast again the next morning, then kissed her like he was a dying man and needed one last breath and said he'd see her later that night.

And he did.

He stopped over with takeout from their favorite Chinese restaurant when they were kids. Oh, man. The food was still as delicious as ever. They made the best egg rolls on the planet.

He did this every night when he didn't have to work— stopped by with takeout—or he made something with the ingredients he'd brought with him. He never expected more from her. Like a kiss. Like sex. Like more sharing of her feelings. He was simply there supporting her.

Sometimes she'd actually spill her guts. Not about the bank robbery, but about things she would never tell another soul. Other times they talked about nothing in particular. A few times, they talked about his family, who married whom from high school and all the juicy gossip she would've devoured when she was eighteen.

It felt like old times.

It felt like they were a couple.

It felt like they could actually rekindle what they'd once had.

Yet, because he didn't make a move, she wasn't sure what to make of his behavior. He said he loved her. He said he'd always love her.

But what did that mean?

Did that mean he wanted to try again at a relationship? Did he really want to remain friends?

The answer frightened her, which prompted her to never ask. Because if she asked and it was the answer she didn't want, she didn't think she'd survive. She was barely surviving as it was.

Her feet met the pavement, step after step, pace after pace. As she ran, thoughts of Ethan and their messed-up relationship—friendship—whatever they wanted to call it, splintered through her mind.

She was so confused, yet blessed.

For the first time since that horrible incident, she was sleeping better at night. She still tossed and turned some-what, but she never woke up in a sweaty mess. And she knew why.

Because of Ethan McCord.

His presence calmed her down. His kindness and under-standing helped her to work through the terror and fear still lingering in her bones.

But how long could she continue this charade? This cover that she only wanted to be friends?

Being just friends was the last thing she wanted.

Like his confession, she still loved him. She'd always love him.

So, where did that leave them?

Her legs ate up the distance as thought after torrential thought jumbled around her mind.

ETHAN KNOCKED ONE MORE TIME, even pushed the doorbell for the third time before slumping his shoulders in defeat. After working all day yesterday and not seeing her beautiful face, he was missing her terribly.

But Penelope wasn't home.

Well, what did he expect? That she waited around patiently for him to stop by?

He didn't make plans with her on what time he'd stop over. He normally appeared, knocking on her door, hoping she'd let him in. Because if he attempted to plan anything with her, she might deny him and he couldn't have that.

So far, she hadn't denied him. She always let him in, and they had a great time catching up and enjoying their time together. It didn't mean he didn't wonder when he got home, tucked away in his bedroom away from prying eyes, how long he'd have to do this song and dance with her.

He wanted to be more than friends. He wanted to wrap her in his arms like he had a right to and love her body all night long. Hell, he'd take simply spending the night in the same bed snuggling together. But he wanted more.

"She left about ten minutes ago. It looked like she was going for a run."

The voice startled him, but he recovered, or at least he thought so, as he turned in the direction of Deja and

Emmett's house. He smiled at Deja, who stood on her doorstep.

"Well, it's a nice day for a run."

Obviously, the sun was shining. What a dumb comment, but he didn't know what else to say. Not to mention, he didn't want to be interrogated by Deja either.

"You've been spending a lot of time over at her house. Are you two...a thing now?"

Oh, they were a thing, all right.

Friends.

So lame, and all his fault saying it in the first place.

Apparently, it didn't matter what he said, even something as stupid as mentioning the weather. If Deja wanted to interrogate him about his relationship with Penelope, which she did, she was going to do it.

"We're friends. I'm being a nice friend and making sure she's doing okay since she was attacked."

And no way in hell he was mentioning the incident in New York. His family was already chomping at the bit to get into his business concerning Penelope; the less ammunition they had about her, the better.

A crafty smile lit up her face. "If you say so. You're more than welcome to hang out here until she gets back. I was just grabbing the mail."

Then, instead of waiting for his response, she headed down the driveway and to the mailbox.

Ethan wasn't sure what he wanted to do. Did he wait with Deja, assuming Emmett was still working? Did he look like an idiot waiting for Penelope on her doorstep? Or did he leave and come back later?

Well, he had been dominating Penelope's time a lot on his off days, and considering he only worked two days in the past week, he was bugging her quite a bit. Maybe she didn't want him to come over every single night when he didn't have to work. They were only friends—at the moment. Hey, he could dream.

He headed for his truck and threw a hand up in good-bye. "I'll swing by later. See ya."

Deja waved, the sly smile still warping her mischievous face.

Backing out of Penelope's driveway, he wasn't sure where he was headed, but he refused to look too eager by waiting in front of her house.

10

PENELOPE WAS BREATHING HEAVILY and barely made it to the front door before collapsing to the ground. Taking a moment on the front stairs of her house to catch her breath, she felt rejuvenated and ready to tackle anything. Opening the water bottle she brought with her, she chugged the contents until it was gone.

Running sure kicked her butt, but it also made her feel more centered and in control of her life. And that's exactly what she needed to do from now on—take control of her life.

Starting with—

Well, that was the problem. She didn't know where to start.

Did she go inside, take a shower, and look for a job?

Or did she go inside, take a shower, and tell Ethan she loved him and wanted to be more than friends?

Because that jog was a real eye-opener. She didn't just pass house after house and scenery after scenery. All her problems and insecurities and worries floated through her mind until she knew it would never clear until she faced each one head on. That included Ethan.

She loved the time they'd been spending together, but she couldn't keep doing this. She couldn't keep pretending she wanted simple friendship. She wanted what she wanted nine years ago.

Marriage. A family. A long, happy life with the man she loved.

So what if they were separated for nine years?

So what if their reunion hadn't gone as well as she planned?

So what if he said he only wanted to be friends?

Maybe he changed his mind. She wouldn't know unless she asked.

The question was, how did she ask him? How did she tell him she wanted more?

Regaining her strength after such a long, hard run, she stood and went inside to take a shower. After she dressed in a comfortable outfit and a light layer of makeup, she sat down at the dining room table with her laptop.

First, she'd find a job. Then she'd find Ethan, or wait for him to show up later, and confess she wanted more.

She didn't have the courage yet to confront him.

Getting down to business, she went searching for a job. Not much was available in St. Joe where she lived, but that didn't matter. St. Cloud wasn't too far away. Finding a few open positions in some private law firms, she spent the rest of the afternoon applying for two jobs.

With the experience she had, especially at one of the biggest law firms in New York City, she had high hopes she'd get at least one of the positions. If not, maybe she'd look into a career change.

Maybe that's what her entire life needed. A whole new change from top to bottom.

After stowing her computer in her bedroom on the nightstand, she walked back to the kitchen and glanced at the time on the microwave—7:59 p.m.

Whoa. The time flew by faster than she realized.

And how odd.

Ethan was usually at her house by now. At least, when he didn't work. She didn't know how he could handle working 24-hour shifts as he did, but when he talked about his job, she always heard the pride and happiness in his tone like it didn't bother him at all.

He didn't give her his work schedule, but he said they usually worked a 24-hour shift then had three days off and then worked another 24-hour shift, and so on. Sometimes it changed here and there, but that was generally his schedule. He worked yesterday, so that meant he should've stopped by today. Not that he needed to show up every day to her house.

Well, it wasn't a big deal he wasn't here yet. Maybe he wasn't coming tonight. He didn't *have* to stop over.

She slowly meandered to the living room, as if that would keep time from shifting forward, before gingerly taking a seat on the couch.

She could make supper.

Or she could wait thirty more minutes for Ethan in case he was still planning on stopping by with food.

She abruptly stood up.

Or she could make supper for him for once. He had been bringing food, whether takeout or ingredients to make a meal. She didn't do anything, although she did help with the dishes. She wasn't completely lazy.

But not tonight.

She'd cook tonight for him.

As long as he showed up.

She wasn't a gourmet cook, but her dad taught her some delicious meals. She didn't think Ethan would care what she made. He could eat just about anything.

Looking through her cupboards and fridge for something yummy to make, she settled on spaghetti and garlic toast.

If he didn't show up tonight, well, then she'd eat on her own. No big deal.

They weren't a couple, after all. He didn't have to come over.

Settling into a rhythm she hadn't had for over a month when cooking a meal for one, she had the spaghetti done within thirty minutes.

Still no Ethan.

She took her time setting the table and placing the food next to the plates.

Still no Ethan.

Her phone glared at her from the kitchen counter, yet she made no move to grab it. She wouldn't call him. If he didn't feel like stopping by, then she wouldn't bother him.

Sitting down in her seat, she loaded her plate with spaghetti and dug in. It didn't take her long to finish her plate and clean up everything, including the dishes.

By the time nine thirty rolled around, she knew he wasn't coming over.

Her enthusiastic mood about confessing she loved him and wanting more than friendship deflated.

He obviously only wanted to be friends. She wouldn't survive his rejection.

Changing into her pajamas, she crawled into bed,

turned off the light and tried to forget how much it hurt to think of remaining only friends.

She couldn't do it.

The next time she saw Ethan McCord, she'd tell him not to come over again.

They couldn't even be friends.

ETHAN KNOCKED on the door and took a step back. He needed a breather before the door opened. His life was about to change—either for better or for worse.

Less than a minute later, it swung open. The look on Penelope's face didn't bode well for him.

He knew it was kind of late to be stopping by, but he had to see her. He had to get it over with, or he'd never sleep tonight.

He had planned to be back at her house by five o'clock, but then he stopped at work to pass the time, and he got distracted with the guys talking about the arsonist. When he left, he started to get cold feet, wondering whether coming to her house was a good idea. Whether expressing his feelings was a good idea. He found himself pacing inside his bedroom, finding the courage to tell her how he really felt.

Here he was, knocking on her door at nearly 11:00 p.m. By the tiredness in her eyes and the see-through tank top and the short shorts she was wearing, she had been sleeping already.

"I woke you up. I'm so sorry."

And he was. What a terrible idea to do this right now. It had been a rough week looking for the serial arsonist; the perp had set another house on fire last night. That had been one reason he'd been so eager to see her earlier. Just to know she was safe. The fire nearly claimed the life of an elderly woman who barely escaped from her burning home. As soon as he laid eyes on the fire roaring high into the night sky, he knew he needed to see Penelope. He needed to know she was okay. Every night before he closed his eyes, he saw Penelope's frightened tearstained face, and he knew he wasn't okay. The only reason he got any sleep at night was because he spent the evening with her. He knew she was okay. There was no way he would've been able to fall asleep tonight without at least seeing her beautiful face.

A tiny smile appeared on her face. "It's fine. It is late, though. Is everything okay?"

"That guy, the one that hurt you last week, he set another house on fire last night. It was a rough night. I just..." He looked away before he blurted out how much he loved her. He couldn't do it. He couldn't confess anything as he planned on the ride over.

"Ethan," she whispered as she grabbed his hand, "come inside."

His gaze rose until he met her beautiful chocolate brown eyes. "He almost killed someone yesterday." His voice lowered as her grip tightened around his hand. "He hurt you."

"But I'm okay." Then she pulled him toward her, and he stepped inside, shutting the door behind him.

"I need..." This time he grabbed her, enfolding her in his arms, getting her as close to him as possible. "I need..."

His mouth lowered, yet stopped short of touching hers. God, he needed to kiss her so badly. He needed to sink into her warm heat. He needed to feel alive and free and like everything was right in his world when he wasn't sure anything would ever be right again.

Yet, he couldn't get out how he wanted to say what he needed.

He just needed her. All of her. Body, heart, and soul.

A soft hand brushed up his cheek and through his hair before trailing down his back. "Well, you said I'd always have you. The same goes for me, Ethan. You'll always have me. Even though..."

He waited for her to finish, maybe she was collecting her thoughts, but she said nothing more.

"Don't stop there. Part of the problem nine years ago was our lack of communication. I should've told you back then how much I loved you and how much I wanted things to work out. I hated when you left. Nine years too late, but there. I said it. If we have something to say, we need to say it. I can handle it."

Her hand behind his back tightened, scrunching his shirt into a ball. "Okay..." She inhaled deeply. "You'll always have me, even though I can't be friends with you anymore."

They still maintained eye contact when her brutal words sliced through the air.

"Can't be friends" was all he heard. Yet, the desire in her eyes told him another story.

"Can we be anything else? I mean, if you don't want to be friends, there are other things we could try." He offered a goofy grin to go along with a very serious question.

The thought of losing her in any capacity was sending him in a tailspin. He came over here tonight to ask her something and now he might lose her forever. Although, with his one question he had yet to ask, he could still lose her.

"I don't know. You're right. We should've communicated better back then. I should've told you how much I didn't want to leave you or lose you in any way. But I also couldn't stay. I would've tried a long-distance relationship." Her eyes fell to his chest. He wouldn't doubt if she could see his heart pounding as if it could jump right out of his chest. "I just can't do friends only with you. I don't know if I can handle anything—"

"Penelope—"

"No, let me finish." A sweet smile lit up her face as she looked back up into his eyes.

He wasn't sure he wanted to let her finish. Especially if it was something he'd hate to hear. He lost nine years with her, and it was the dumbest thing he ever did letting her walk away when he didn't have to. He wasn't going to repeat his mistakes.

"I can't handle anything less than a real relationship. One where we talk about the future...marriage, even. I want a family. I want kids. But I don't want to be just friends when it hurts to think I want more from you. I told myself I wouldn't say anything because I didn't want to ruin anything between us, but there it is. That's what I want. If we can't try it, then that's okay, but I can't be just friends."

His rapidly beating heart wanted to slow down and whoop for joy, but it maintained its eager, erratic pace. Because, although she said what he hoped she'd say, he had no idea how she'd react to his next question. Maybe he was jumping the gun.

Digging into his pocket, he pulled out a ring and held it up between them. A tiny gasp left her lips as soon as she eyed the cheap twenty-five cent sapphire ring he bought for her at the mall out of one of the machines when they were only eighteen years old. Well, he sort of bought it for her. He actually put a quarter in the machine to get her a gumball and out popped a tiny plastic container with the ring. It's as if it had always been meant to be between them.

"Remember when I bought this for you, and I joked one day I'd ask you to marry me with this exact ring?"

She nodded, her eyes filling with water.

"I tossed it into my wallet and said I'd pull it out when I was ready. It's been in my wallet since that day." He pulled her closer when he started to feel a slight tremble in her body. "I thought I'd pull it out on our graduation day, but that didn't happen. But I'm pulling it out now. I love you, Penelope. I always have, and I always will. Nine years, cities apart, nothing will ever stop my love. I'm sorry I was an idiot for so long. I swear I'll try harder from here on out."

"Oh, Ethan." A lone tear slid down her cheek.

"Will you marry me, Penelope? And if you need—want —to move somewhere else, I'll go. Wherever you are, I am. I lost nine years with you. I don't want to lose any more."

Another tear slid down as she leaned closer and kissed him. "Yes, Ethan. I will marry you. But I don't want to move. This is home."

It was home for him, too, but he'd do anything for her.

She was his home.

Always.

THE TEARS WOULDN'T SUBSIDE as Ethan slid the cheap ring onto her finger. She honestly didn't think she had any tears left inside, but apparently, she was wrong. Oh, these were the best kind of tears. Happy, happy tears. She never would've imagined returning home and finding herself back in Ethan's arms.

"I hate when you cry. Why are you crying still?" Ethan asked as he wiped a few tears from her cheeks.

Her eyes lifted from her finger to his handsome, adoring

face. "Because I've never been so happy in my life. I know we've been through so much, but I know now we can get through anything." Then she tapped him on the chest with a stern smile. "As long as we continue to talk things through. If this is going to work, we can't act like we did back then. We need to communicate."

He swiped a few more tears away before wrapping his arms around her waist. "I might be a work in progress, but I promise to try my best. I swear I will do everything in my power to make you happy and make this work."

Then he lifted her up. She let out a surprised laugh as she wrapped her legs around his waist.

"Since we're working on our communication, then I need to tell you I'm about to make sweet love to you. That I can't keep my hands to myself any longer. It's killing me not being deep inside you." A brilliant smile lit up his face. "How's that for communicating?"

Her legs tightened around his waist as she brushed her fingers through his silky, black hair. "It's definitely a good start."

She showered him with kisses as he made his way to her bedroom. Another round of laughter fell from her lips when he tossed her lightly on the bed. He was naked a few seconds later, getting undressed quickly, telling her exactly how much he wanted her. Maybe they didn't need words to express how they felt all the time. She could see how much he loved her by the way his eyes devoured her, by his soft touch as he removed her clothes.

She loved this man so much, she wasn't sure how she survived the past nine years without him in her life. But it didn't matter how because she had him now.

When he had removed her panties and slid on top of her, his mouth didn't hesitate to capture hers. The kiss was

slow and tender, conveying his love in each small movement. He had never kissed her so exquisitely before—as if
she were a prized treasure centuries old needing the
tenderest touch.

"More, Ethan. I need more of you," she whispered
against his lips, desperate to feel more of his loving touch in
other places.

His hand slid slowly down her side, gripping her hip in a
possessive manner as he arched into her body. "We have all
night, Penelope. I want to savor this moment." Then he
ground against her again, her body instantly begging for
more. "But I need more, too." The kiss suddenly turned hard
and intense. "So much more."

Her hands tightened in his hair, digging and pulling as
their lips tangled together in a heap of explosive energy.
God, she loved this man with every bit of her soul.

He broke the kiss for a brief moment to grab a condom
and donned it quickly, then his lips met hers once again as
he slid deep inside. A sigh of contentment left both of their
mouths.

Then he started to move.

"I love you, Penelope Justice. Always and forever."

Her hands smoothed through his hair and to his back
where she held on for what she knew would be a wild ride
when his thrusts became harder and stronger.

"Oh, I love you more, Ethan McCord. Always and
forever."

The intensity, the passion, the ecstasy building in the
room didn't take long to pique. The love between them
exploded with such ardor that she never wanted the feeling
to end. Even after the bliss started to dissipate, she held onto
him, never wanting to let go.

He felt the same way because his body didn't move an

inch, except for his lips that placed light kisses everywhere from her neck to her mouth.

Then his gorgeous brown eyes met hers. "I'll buy you a real ring tomorrow. I promise."

She felt the cheap sapphire ring wrapped around her finger and smiled. "I would marry you with this ring on my finger. It's not the ring that means something, it's the memory."

A deep, thorough kiss touched her lips. "Then you get two rings because I'm still buying you another one. You deserve it. You deserve everything, Penelope. I swear I'll give it all to you."

As long as he continued to give all his love, she didn't need anything else.

She had everything she already needed.

EPILOGUE

PENELOPE HALF RAN to the door when the doorbell went off. She swiped her witch hat from the little side table next to the door before opening it. When she opened the door, expecting to see an adorable kid dressed up in a great costume, she started laughing at what she actually saw.

"Trick or Treat," Emmett said with a beaming smile as he held out a large empty orange bowl with a pumpkin face on the side.

Gabe stood quietly next to him. He nodded at her but said nothing. She wasn't surprised. Since the night of the bar fiasco, he hadn't said much to her, the little she saw of him as if she had done something wrong that night. But she hadn't. They hadn't been laughing at Ethan, and he knew that. She only wished Gabe believed it.

They were getting married now. No date set, but they'd been engaged for two weeks, and everything was going so well. They hadn't decided who was moving in with whom, but so far he'd been staying at her house a lot. They had planned to hand out candy together for Halloween, but he said he needed to run home for something and he'd be back in a little bit. Although, he had called about ten minutes ago and said he'd be on his way soon.

"Come on in." Penelope held the door open wider and glanced at his bowl as they stepped through the threshold, then closed the door behind them. "Am I supposed to fill that entire bowl?"

"Who knew the kids were so ravenous this year? We already ran out of candy. I blame Deja. She's been giving out handfuls. I told her only two pieces, if that, from now on. Do you have a few extra we can borrow?"

"Sure. We'll split what I have, and I'll call Ethan to swing by the store to grab more. I'll tell him to buy plenty so Deja can continue giving handfuls. Where's the fun if you don't get a handful of candy?"

Emmett chuckled, then winked. "You're right, and it sure puts a smile on her face." Emmett turned to Gabe and handed him the bowl. "I have to use the bathroom. I can't hold it. I thought I could."

Penelope laughed as he raced down the hallway. "Was he watching Deja like a hawk about the candy that he didn't go before he walked over here?"

"Something like that," Gabe said quietly, then eyed the bowl of candy sitting on her little side table she found at a garage sale for only fifty cents.

She took that as her cue that Gabe didn't want to talk and started to divvy up the candy between them.

"There you go." She smiled as friendly as she could when she finished the quick task. Her heart started to lightly pound.

Oh, boy. Her episodes, as she liked to call them, hadn't been as bad lately. She didn't talk about what happened again to Ethan, but that small purge of her emotions helped. And so did running every day. She tried to run, rain or shine, cold or hot, not that October got too hot, but she tried to go for a run around the neighborhood every day. It helped her. It helped to release the anguish and despair that had been festering and building since that terrible nightmare occurred. Although the serial arsonist hadn't been caught yet, she refused to let that keep her hidden inside either.

But it didn't mean she didn't have moments of anxiety every now and again. She still refused to believe she had panic attacks.

Gabe nodded and surprisingly offered a small grin. "Thank you. This wasn't a two-man job."

Very true, but even if she'd thought so, she never would've pointed it out. Considering she didn't know how to respond, she didn't. Instead, her heart rate kicked up a notch. Maybe that's why it originally started to thud like a jackhammer going wild. Because she knew Gabe was about to say something she wouldn't like.

"I apologize if I haven't been overly friendly. It has nothing to do with you. I've been..." His eyes turned to the floor. "I've been distracted lately with some stuff, and it's a bit stressful." Then his eyes found hers once more. "I'm happy for you both. Welcome to the family, Penelope."

Because she couldn't control the erratic emotions going off inside her, her hands started to tremble and her eyes filled with tears.

"Oh, man. Don't cry—"

Before he could say more, she threw her arms around him, jostling the bowl in his arms, making a few pieces of candy jump out of the bowl and to the floor.

"Thank you, Gabe. I don't know what's wrong with me. But you don't know how much I appreciate hearing that." She didn't want to embarrass herself any longer, so she stepped back and wiped her eyes dry. "I thought you hated me."

"I definitely don't hate you. I have a lot going on in my head, and I took it out on you. I'm sorry."

To distract herself, especially by the compassionate and sincere look in his eyes, she bent down and picked up the candy that fell. Then she stood up, more composed, and tossed it back into his bowl.

"If you ever need me, I'm here for you. I can be a good listener."

"Thank you." Then he smiled and jiggled the bowl. "We're set for another five minutes."

Penelope turned slightly when she heard Emmett laugh.

"With Deja, we'll be lucky if it lasts five minutes." Emmett gave her a small side hug, then opened the door. "Thank you. We appreciate it, and so do the kids."

She said goodbye and called Ethan to grab more candy. Then she continued her routine of answering the door handing out candy and running back to the kitchen to finish making supper.

She and Ethan had gotten in the habit of taking turns when he didn't have to work making something to eat. Since her day landed on Halloween, she decided to make a jack-o-lantern pot pie and a cherry pie with the top shaped like the face of a zombie. Ethan loved cherry pie. The entire thing would probably be consumed tonight.

After rinsing the last dirty dish and wiping her hands, she turned around to check the timer and screamed as if a madman stood before her with a knife coated in dripping blood.

Ethan busted out laughing until she couldn't control herself and joined in the laughter.

Slapping his shoulder, she chided him. "You scared me to death. Make a little noise next time."

"Where's the fun in that?" Ethan asked with a devilish smile, then pulled her into his arms and kissed her lightly on the lips.

Her fingers felt sticky from slapping him on the shoulder. They were stained with something red.

"What is all this red stuff on you?"

"Blood."

Cocking a brow, she chuckled. "Yes, it looks like blood, but what is it actually?"

She hadn't expected him to come home dressed in his costume, especially since he left without a costume on. But he was ready for the festivities looking like the best zombie she had ever seen. Gory face makeup, tattered clothes, and blood smeared everywhere.

"Ketchup and whatever else Dare and I had in the house. I thought I'd surprise you."

"Oh, you surprised me, all right."

Ethan delivered a few more delightful kisses before the doorbell went off, and they were back at it handing out candy. She asked about Emmett's candy, and Ethan said he already dropped it off next door. Such a good thing because the next half hour was busy with kid after kid ringing the doorbell. Ethan picked up several large bags of candy, so she made sure to give the biggest handful to each excited little kid who walked up to the door. Just like Deja was doing.

When her timer went off, she took a quick break to pull the pot pie out of the oven, then set the table. They were able to eat their meal with not too many interruptions because it was getting later in the evening. Of course, Ethan devoured two slices of the cherry pie, even saying he'd be coming back for more later before bedtime.

When they finally turned off the porch light and picked everything up, they barely had three handfuls of candy left in the bowl.

All in all, she'd say it was a good Halloween celebration.

Ethan grabbed her around the waist after she set the candy bowl on the dining room table and kissed her on the lips.

"What did the zombie say to the witch?"

She chuckled, thinking hard. He loved to tell jokes in high school, and some did have her laughing so hard, tears would stream down her face. Other times, she shook her head at how lame they were.

But nothing was popping in her head with this one. Zombies didn't talk.

"I have no idea," she said with a short laugh.

His mouth drew near hers, as his hands tightened on her waist. "I'm going to devour you from head to toe."

Ah, wasn't he a clever one. It wasn't a bad joke and had her chuckling. "If zombies could talk, they might say that. Or 'I'm gonna eat you.'"

Ethan swooped her into his arms, his eyes shimmering with passion. "I thought my version was less abrasive, but yes, I am going to enjoy every little morsel in my arms."

She rested her head on his shoulder as he carried her to the bathroom to shower first. Oh, she knew exactly what would happen. They'd enjoy their time in the shower, wash every inch of each other, then the fun would head to the bedroom where Ethan would do the most amazing and delicious things to her—and vice versa. She loved exploring his body and finding new spots that made him groan and growl for more.

Nine years ago, her heart splintered into a million pieces.

Now, she realized, they had an always kind of love. The kind that never died, no matter the obstacle.

Ethan showed her every day that it was true.

Don't miss the next book in this angsty, yet heartwarming series! You find out who the arsonist is as well!

Finding You

FOR ZANE & AVA'S STORY
PROTECTING YOU
A MCCORD FAMILY NOVEL, #1

He wanted to hate her.
She needed his forgiveness.
Love has a way of healing even the deepest wounds.

Zane McCord has always been there for his brothers, no matter what. But when his brother Jimmy dies, leaving unresolved tension hanging between them, he turns all his hatred and blame onto Ava Rainer— the woman he holds responsible for Jimmy's death. He doesn't want anything to do with her, but when she unexpectedly shows up on his farm, needing his help, Zane finds himself drawn to her, despite every effort to push her away.

Ava can't escape the guilt weighing heavy on her shoulders, and she's desperate to make amends. Working together gives her the perfect opportunity to break down the walls he's built around his heart and set them both on a journey of forgiveness, healing, and unexpected love. But with the painful memories of the past looming, can they ever truly move forward and find happiness in each other's arms, or will the guilt prove too much and destroy everything?

*Grab your copy of **Protecting You** today and witness the power of forgiveness and love.*

FOR AUSTIN & SOPHIE'S STORY
TRUST IN LOVE
A MCCORD FAMILY NOVEL, #2

He wasn't looking for love.
She was afraid to trust again.
When fate brings them together, will they take a chance on
forever?

Austin McCord has always enjoyed the company of women, but he's never been one for commitment. Until he meets his neighbor, Sophie. With her angelic face and kind heart, she's everything he never knew he wanted. But there's a catch—Sophie is the type that has marriage written all over her, making her untouchable.

Despite his best efforts, the temptation proves too much. Austin is drawn to Sophie like a moth to a flame, but every time he tries to get close, she pulls away. It's obvious that she's been hurt before, and for the first time in his life, Austin finds himself in hot pursuit.

As he tries to break down her walls, the past looms ahead, threatening to tear them apart. With danger closing in, Austin finds himself fighting for not only Sophie's heart but also her safety.

Will they find the courage to take a leap of faith on love before it's ripped away from them forever?

Fall in love with Austin and Sophie's story today and discover if they can overcome their fears and forge a future together.

FOR EMMETT & DEJA'S STORY
DESERVING YOU
A MCCORD FAMILY NOVEL, #3

She doesn't think she's worthy of his love.
He knows she's the only one for him.
But the ghosts of her past could shatter any chance they have at
happiness.

Emmett McCord has been captivated by Deja from the start, despite the circumstances that brought her into his family's world. Her strength, determination, and unwavering loyalty make it easy to forgive, but Deja's fear and self-doubt threaten to push Emmett away.

He can't risk losing their friendship, but when Deja's brother, the only person she's ever trusted and known love from, is released from prison, Emmett can no longer stay silent. Her brother doesn't want to stick around and Deja's determined to follow him. Can he find a way to break through Deja's walls and prove to her the depth of his love before she runs again?

Don't miss this emotional journey of love and redemption. Grab your copy of **Deserving You** *today and discover if Emmett and Deja can overcome the past to build a future together!*

FOR GABE & OLIVIA'S STORY
FINDING YOU
A McCORD FAMILY NOVEL, #5

What happens in Vegas doesn't always stay in Vegas. One wild mishap could be the best thing that ever happened to him.

Being shy makes it hard for Gabe McCord to talk to women, but throw in a fun, wild night of drinking and it's not so hard. Until he learns he didn't just wake up next to a gorgeous woman—he married her. Nine months later and he's still trying to find her...when she accidentally finds him.

Olivia Brenson is the new arson investigator in town trying to find the person responsible for multiple fires, the latest one which almost took a life. When she learns they're married—because neither remembered their nuptials—Gabe finds himself on another fun adventure. She wants to stay married for a short time to keep her overprotective, demanding father off her back. He doesn't protest as it gives him a chance to prove he isn't always the shy guy. But if he's not careful, he might lose more than just his reserved tendencies. He'll lose his heart along the way. Because he's finding Olivia is the woman he never knew he needed in his life.

With nail-biting suspense and smoldering romance, dive into the danger and desire with Gabe & Olivia's story!

For Dare & Julie's story
Dare You to Love
A McCord Family Novel, #6

He's looking for a fresh start.
She only wants to unwind and relax.
But when opposites attract, anything can happen.

He's done his time, but once a felon, always a felon. Nobody lets him forget that. Dare needs to leave town, get a new start somewhere else where no one knows him and what he's done. If only it were that simple. Not only is it impossible to find the right time to tell his sister he's hitting the road, he meets a woman who gets under his skin without even trying. There's something about her that he can't resist. And she knows it. So when he's asked to do something that could send him spiraling back into his old life, he wants to say no. He wants to run in the opposite direction and never stop. If only she'd let him.

Vacation time is meant to relax, not bring the stress and tension bearing down on her. Of course, meeting a man who challenges her in so many ways, well, Julie can't ignore that. Nor can she combat the desire that attacks her body every time he looks her way. Fighting comes easy to them, and so does the pleasure. It should be just sex, yet it's turning into more than she bargained for. It would never work between them. She works for the law, and he...is only trying to find a new path, and she respects that. If only it were that easy.

ABOUT THE AUTHOR

I'm a *USA Today* Bestselling Author that loves to write contemporary romance and romantic suspense novels, although I am partial to romantic suspense. I even dabble in paranormal. Honestly, I love anything that has to do with romance. As long as there's a happy ending, I'm a happy camper. And insta-love...yes, please! I love baseball (Go Twins!) and creating awesome crafts. I graduated with a Bachelor's Degree in Criminal Justice, working in that field for several years before I became a stay-at-home mom. I have a few more amazing stories in the works. If you would like to learn more about me and my books, head to my website by scanning the QR code. Thanks for reading!

Scan me

www.ingramcontent.com/pod-product-compliance
Lightning Source LLC
Chambersburg PA
CBHW051927240626
47153CB00004B/1399